D0331437

THE LOST MANUSCRIPT

ALSO BY CATHY BONIDAN

The Perfume of the Hellebore Rose

THE LOST MANUSCRIPT

Cathy Bonidan

Translated from the French
by Emma Ramadan

ST. MARTIN'S PRESS
New York

First published in the United States by St. Martin's Press, an imprint of St. Martin's Publishing Group

THE LOST MANUSCRIPT. Copyright © 2019 by Cathy Bonidan. English translation copyright © 2021 by Emma Ramadan. All rights reserved. Printed in the United States of America. For information, address St. Martin's Publishing Group, 120 Broadway, New York, NY 10271.

Design by Donna Sinisgalli Noetzel

www.stmartins.com

The Library of Congress Cataloging-in-Publication Data is available upon request.

ISBN 978-1-250-25630-0 (hardcover)
ISBN 978-1-250-25631-7 (ebook)

Our books may be purchased in bulk for promotional, educational, or business use. Please contact your local bookseller or the Macmillan Corporate and Premium Sales Department at 1-800-221-7945, extension 5442, or by email at MacmillanSpecialMarkets@macmillan.com.

Originally published in France in 2019 under the title *Chambre 128* by Éditions de La Martinière

First U.S. Edition: 2021

10 9 8 7 6 5 4 3 2 1

To all the books we've read.

To all those we have yet to read.

Because like sandmen,

they sprinkle into our daily lives

a few words or phrases

that work their way into our subconscious over time.

And change us.

Discreetly, but irrevocably.

This is a true story. Or almost...

When we happen to witness a slice of life that occurs before our eyes, we have very little power over where it leads. We observe the protagonists and imagine their feelings, their fears, their hopes.

Of course, sometimes we are wrong.

But we often feel close to the truth and charged with a mission: to recount, one day at a time, the events that we've observed. Of course, if we do this, we risk being surprised by the outcome.

And what if the ending disappoints us?

It's a possibility.

So, if you accept this risk, if you appreciate uncertainty, read these letters, one by one, submitting to the peaceful and unpredictable rhythm of mail delivery . . .

Only the places and the names of characters have been changed.

THE LOST MANUSCRIPT

from Anne-Lise Briard

Dear Madam or Sir,

I am sending you this package very late, please forgive me.

After discovering it in room 128, someone else would have im-mediately handed it over to the reception of the Beau Rivage Hotel; nevertheless, if you were to ask those who know me, they'd tell you just how lazy I can be in my daily life. So don't take this post-ponement to mean that I don't like your book. Not at all. I will even admit to you: I read it.

I had just opened the nightstand to the right of the double bed, which as it happens was quite comfortable, when I was delighted to find the distraction you provided me. You see, I had forgotten to bring a novel to keep me company this weekend on the shore of the Iroise Sea . . . Since I can't fall asleep without first reading a few pages, I become very annoying when I'm deprived of the pleasure. Thanks to you, my husband didn't have to deal with my rotten mood.

Anyway, it was on page 156 that I found—between two chapters—the address to where I'm sending these pages. I hesitated for a long time and, to tell you the truth, my spouse and my children didn't support my "bizarre" initiative—to use my daughter's vocabulary, her only excuse being that she's sixteen years old.

My husband decided it must be an old manuscript turned down by publishing houses and abandoned in a drawer, waiting to attract some desperate reader. My son went even further, arguing that a book in such a bad state and typed on a primitive typewriter must have been lying around in that hotel "for eons" and that its owner would have retrieved it "ages ago" if it held even the slightest interest in their eyes.

I was almost convinced by their arguments, until I arrived at page 164. There, in the margin, was this note:

What's the point in the end? Don't lies eventually lead us to the path of truth? And don't my stories, true or false, come to the same conclusion, don't they all have the same meaning? So what does it matter if they're true or false if, in both cases, they signify what I have been and what I am. Sometimes we see more clearly into someone who lies than into someone who tells the truth.

I was so surprised to see that quote! I had stumbled upon an anonymous author by chance and discovered that he also was an admirer of my favorite writer. By stealing these few sentences from him, you reinforced the ambiguity of your text. While I was wondering at page 164 whether I was reading fiction or someone's life story, you sent me, in an aside, a response from Normand . . .

And then I discovered the poems on the last page, added in pencil, in a slanted handwriting covered with traces of eraser, evidence that someone had deliberated over the right words. Let me assure you that you succeeded. When I read your words, I felt that slight shiver we feel when the lines we're reading seem to have been written just for us.

It was at that moment, I think, that I decided to thumb my nose at my family's advice and return the book, without knowing whether I was sending it to a woman, a man, a teenager, or an elderly person, lugging the manuscript from hotel to hotel, like those believers who protect themselves from the wrath of God by carrying a Bible wherever they go.

The only way to get a response was to entrust the package to the postal services, hoping a creative mailman would track you down at the end of the journey (having never sent a package with an address but no addressee, I'm counting on the amused curiosity of an underpaid employee to help me carry out this return).

If you would be so kind as to acknowledge receipt, you'll find my name and address on the back of the envelope.

Thank you for the enjoyable reading experience you've provided me, even if unwittingly.

Sincerely,

Anne-Lise Briard

from *Sylvestre Fahmer to Anne-Lise Briard*

LES CHAYETS, LAINVILLE-EN-VEXIN, MAY 2, 2016

I've just finished reading your letter for the tenth time . . . How can I say this so that you'll understand? This manuscript . . . it would take so long to explain. And your letter . . . written by hand and for me alone, reminding me of the letters I received as a child when I was away at summer camp. My mother had that same rushed and slanted handwriting, as if she were trying to recount as much as possible before the mailman arrived. She loved to write and only had the opportunity to do so occasionally. My being away served as an excuse for her to devote herself to that pointless activity, which was put down by everyone around her. Like you, she used terms that were obsolete, practically prohibited, convinced that a fountain pen required more than the everyday lexicon. How she would have appreciated your *postponement, thumb my nose,* and *as it happens*! We don't hear those phrases anymore, especially not in the impersonal and intrusive e-mails that inundate our virtual mailboxes . . .

So today, once again, I savor the joy and diligence I poured into the responses to my mother, even though I was eager to catch the spelling errors and the vague vocabulary she would always scold me for upon my return. I hope you'll be more indulgent than she was and keep in mind that I'm out of practice.

I just got your package last night: the address you found belongs to my godfather, who, fortunately, still resides in the same place he's lived in for the last fifty years . . .

He was formerly a distinguished chef and it was very difficult for him to accept going into retirement and saying good-bye to his stovetop. That's why, every Friday night, in his little eighth-floor apartment, he invites a group of regulars to come try out his new culinary inventions. Given that he's ninety-two years old and has less than perfect vision, you'll understand why it's only the adventurous who accept his invitation . . . Because the mailman is a devotee of the gourmet, unconventional meals organized by my godfather, he's very familiar with the building and its occupants. So it was easy for him—and even enjoyable—to investigate. After opening the package—and reading the first few pages of the book—he wasted no time making his way through the eight floors of the building to question all the tenants until he finally matched a recipient to that orphan address.

Luckily, my godfather remembered my long-ago writing attempts. He placed the precious package on his dresser and let it gather a layer of dust before he decided to give me a call.

Believe it or not, when I opened it, I could almost smell the salty sea air and hear the rumbling of the surf and the shrieking of the gulls. That feeling has stayed with me since and I'm all the more surprised because I'm not familiar with that region of Brittany where you say you found it. I have never been particularly fond of the sea and, generally speaking, avoid trips and all the disruptions they entail.

So that you'll understand just how extraordinary your find is: I lost this manuscript on April 3, 1983, on a trip to Montreal. With the arrogance of my twenty-three years, I was hoping to get some writing advice from an acquaintance who was also a well-known literary critic. To show you how much I appreciate the marvelous gift you've given me, but also to prove your son right, I'll admit that I searched for it for months, even questioning the airline and the various people who might have found it. I wrote to the stewards and the flight attendants, as well as the cleaners. I spoke to the shop-keepers in the Montreal airport, and also those in the Paris airport when I returned from my trip. I hoped that a passenger might have left it in a café, or sent it back to the critic whose name was on the envelope. No such luck! I was forced to say good-bye to my first manuscript, which, after that misadventure, was also my last.

And there you have it! Thirty-three years later, you pull it out of a nightstand in a room overlooking the sea, nestled in a hotel in Finistère . . . But I have to tell you something even more incredible: the original work ended on page 156, where you found my god-father's address. At the time, I was living with other students and I was afraid they would mock my literary aspirations if the book was sent back to me.

Maybe if you'd known that, you would have noticed that start-ing on page 157, the style becomes more fluid. My successor was not content merely to finish my book; it seems that on top of it, they did so with a certain artistry.

I am also not the author of the poems in the margins . . . They must belong to the mystery person who discovered my manuscript, probably under an airplane seat, and took it upon themselves to finish it before abandoning it at the very tip of Brittany. That man (or that woman, since we have no way of knowing) was not thoughtful enough to send me their additions as you have done.

In the years that followed, from time to time I wondered what my life would have been like if I hadn't lost that manuscript. I imagined rolling the dice of destiny again, brilliantly finishing the book, pitching it to an editor, and experiencing the dazzling ascent of a young writer praised by the literati . . . As you can see, I entertained these unfulfilled, adolescent dreams for a long time.

Speaking of unfulfilled, you didn't say anything about the story! What am I supposed to think about your silence? A stranger returns this manuscript to me, even though she is under no obligation, thanks me for a pleasant read, reveals implicitly that she's passionate about literature, and yet doesn't even tell me what she thinks . . .

Never mind, forget I said anything. And thank you for sending me these few lines that will keep me company from now on, like the nostalgia of a bygone youth.

Sylvestre Fahmer

P.S. I noticed that you slipped the card of the Beau Rivage Hotel into your package; I'll be sure to book a room there should reckless footsteps lead me to the area one day.

P.P.S. I hope you'll forgive my shaky handwriting. I tried my best, but clearly I haven't had much chance to practice since my summer camp days . . .

from Anne-Lise to Sylvestre

Dear Sylvestre,

Thank you for letting me know that you received that rather peculiar package. Now I feel as though I've done a good deed and that makes me happy, as it does most people. Like your mother, I have a particular tenderness for epistolary exchanges. For a long time now I haven't had the opportunity to use my stationery and people respond to my cards by e-mail, or worse, by text. You might notice that I've set aside the phone number you sent me so that I could send this letter to your actual address, which conjures up images of the French countryside.

You asked to know my opinion as a reader and I will share it with you. First of all, I was moved by the plot. The narrative could have been sappy, but it's not. Good feelings abound but, told from the perspective of a man and spoiled with so many inaccuracies on the nature of women, it's rather refreshing. And the nostalgic reflections, sprinkled here and there by young people, give us a feeling of urgency as if we were embarking on a new day knowing it might be the last. Now that I know that you are responsible only for the first part, I can admit to you without lying that I was disappointed by the ending.

Certainly, as you humbly said, the second half gains fluidity. The style is more striking and sophisticated. The descriptions are written with poetic subtlety without ever stopping the rhythm of the plot and there is a professionalism in the editing that I didn't see at the beginning of the book . . . I can be honest about all of this without fear of offending you, because I believe that skill does a disservice to your text. I lost my emotional connection to it in the same way that perfection in a person lessens their charm. I think you'll understand what I mean.

In summary, the book's first author introduced a candor and a sensibility that gave me chills, while the second furnished it with a linguistic excellence that would delight a French professor.

If I can give you a piece of advice—and this is merely a formality because I won't wait for your agreement: finish it! Take back your story and your right to give it its true ending.

The annotation added by our second author (excuse me for this possessive when I have nothing to do with this story) shows that he appropriated your manuscript. That he entered into it without permission and granted it an ending worthy of admiration, of course, but quite different, I'm certain, from the one you would have chosen. While I write you these few sentences, I'm dreaming of what such a meeting could produce: you, the man with the wounded sensibility and sensitive skin, and he, the brilliant storyteller, capable of placing the right word in the right place without fail. But some meetings are not meant to take place and the world is therefore deprived of potential masterpieces . . .

There you have it, dear Sylvestre, my opinion as a reader. I hope that this will help you to complete your book, for the things we leave unfinished stay with us all our lives like chronic pain that resists the strongest painkillers.

Hoping to read your work again one day, for it is never too late to publish.

Best wishes,

Anne-Lise

from Anne-Lise to Maggy

Dear Maggy,

I hope the "grown-ups" cleaned up your house before heading back to the city . . . I know how annoying it is not to find your things in their place when you come back after a long time away. During the few days we spent in the area, I did everything I could to keep an eye on their outings and their visitors, but you know how skilled they are at avoiding my vigilance . . . I was pretty worried when we abandoned your home to them, even for a short three-day period!

Anyway, they came back delighted with their new independence and say thank you. As for the adults, we took advantage of the sea air and the impeccable service at the hotel you recommended. It is so rare for a mother to feel like she's on vacation!

Speaking of that hotel, I have a favor to ask you. During our stay in room 128 with the superb view you're so familiar with, I discovered a forgotten manuscript in the nightstand. At the time, it was amusing, but nothing exceptional, and you will not be surprised to learn that I sent it back to its owner.

That's where things took an interesting turn: it turns out that the author in question had not finished his story and the ending was in fact written by a stranger, perhaps the person who stayed in room 128 before me. In your opinion, what is the likelihood that two writers who have never met could unite their talents to create a cohesive work?

You've likely guessed what I'm about to ask . . . Could you, calling on your friendship with the hotel manager, find the contact information of the person who stayed in the room before us? The manager will surely cite the confidentiality guests rightly expect from such an establishment. But if you cannot manage to convince her, who else can? I'm not trying to flatter you, but rather to express my genuine admiration for your ability to persuade others.

I hope we'll be able to see each other before the summer. I can't wait to hear the stories from your trip and your thoughts on the countries you visited.

Talk to you soon.

Your friend,

Lisou

P.S. The situation isn't getting any better at the office. If you found a terrible poison in any of those distant countries that would pass undetected in an autopsy, send me a barrel of the miraculous product . . . My hatred for Bastien has only increased since my return and it's time for this rivalry to officially come to an end!

from Sylvestre to Anne-Lise

LES CHAYETS, MAY 9, 2016

I didn't expect to hear back from you so quickly, and the fact that you prefer to communicate by letter makes me want to write you back on the spot. To tell you the truth, for the last two years, I've turned off the ringer on my phone, which goes to an answering machine that serves as a buffer. I have an insatiable need for silence.

Tonight the house is empty, and I can breathe more deeply when I'm alone. My partner is always running from one activity to another without ever taking a breath and, right now, she's on her way from a gymnastics class to a rehearsal for her theater club to a meeting for an events committee, or perhaps she's enjoying dinner at a restaurant with one of her friends. Believe me, her busy schedule has guaranteed the longevity of our relationship more than all the therapy we could have had.

You read my only book, so you must have noticed my desire for calm and idleness. My wife's absence allows me to satisfy both of those needs. As for our daughter, she's left the nest, as they say, and she flies on her own two wings at the other end of the world, or almost, because she lives in Canada . . . I know you didn't ask me about my family, but knowing a bit about yours, I thought it would be a good idea to put us on equal footing.

For the past few days, following your advice, I have brought my manuscript into the twenty-first century. Yes, yes, you read that correctly. I've returned to the first part that I'd written on an old typewriter, which is currently enjoying a well-deserved retirement in a collector's attic. The act of placing my fingers on a computer keyboard and seeing the text appear in this new format renders the story strange to me, almost distant, like in the early morning when we recall a dream that troubled our night. I'm choosing this metaphor because my little naïve, ridiculous story has nothing of the great fanciful epics that have impacted generations of readers. Nevertheless, it merits a certain homage after all the time it's been in my thoughts.

Now I'm rediscovering it through your eyes and I forgive you for using the term "sappy," which, even though it did upset me, is nevertheless justified. I am astonished at the pages I wrote that seem to be straight out of a Harlequin romance book, when I was already old enough to be considered a "man" and no longer a "teenager." But you are right, that innocence lends the story an impression of involvement, of closeness. I'm sure there are many of us who are still holding on to the memory of interrupted love affairs, left dreaming of what might have come next, unable to live it.

You told me to continue writing and I hope you realize you are responsible for this. I'll take advantage of this to ask for your help: Will you read my new work once I've finished it?

I'll understand if you refuse. Without knowing you, I can already imagine you raising your eyebrows as you read these lines, disapproving of my audacity. I would react in the same way if our roles were reversed . . .

Sylvestre

P.S. You mentioned that I am ignorant when it comes to the nature of women . . . what do you mean by that?

POINTE DES RENARDS, LE CONQUET, MAY 13, 2016

Hi, my Lisou!

Can you tell me more about this new project you're talking about now? Tell me all about your plans, which remind me of the adventures we would have when we were ten years old, both of us corrupted by the characters of Enid Blyton.

I was thrilled to put back on my detective cap, and immediately went to see Agathe, as you asked. She is, of course, a die-hard fan of Agatha Christie and gave me no trouble when I asked for the name of the person who stayed in the room before you. To preserve the reputation of her hotel, I advised her to contact the occupant herself to ask permission.

Almost immediately we discovered that the young man was at the hotel with his fiancée for just one night and confessed that he hadn't taken the time to leaf through the book, though he noticed it in the nightstand. Our two lovebirds didn't remove it from its hiding place and didn't deem it necessary to mention to the front desk . . . They apologized for not doing so and Agathe assured them they had done nothing wrong.

Don't be upset, Lisou, you know how determined I am . . . And so we called the woman who was in room 128 just before the young couple. It turns out that this person is ready to swear on the Bible (or on any other book important enough to have a leather cover) that there was no manuscript in her room. She stayed there for a week and made herself quite at home. A big bookworm, she had tucked her reading provisions into the two nightstands, which were empty upon her arrival.

Agathe, our Sherlock Holmes in a petticoat, promised to gather all her staff tomorrow morning to question the potential witnesses and solve this mystery. Now I have turned into Doctor Watson, and so I will send you a full report of what happens at this unusual meeting. I have no other updates at the moment, but be assured that the Breton detectives are on the case and will provide you with the conclusion of the story, even if it means missing sleep or another of their usual activities, such as catching sea snails or eating *galettes-saucisses*.

Your comrade,

Maggy

P.S. I found my house in perfect condition and I applaud your children and their friends for having tidied up so well. Do you know that they even left me a bouquet of flowers on the living room table? They've dried, of course, but it still makes for a lovely decoration!

P.P.S. Forget about Bastien! He's not worth risking prison over . . . Try humiliating him instead! You know that old piece of advice for defusing conflict: imagine your adversary completely naked while he gives a speech in front of his audience. But around here, we have something more effective: add to that birthday suit a Bigouden headdress and you'll feel better, guaranteed!

RUE DES MORILLONS, MAY 14, 2016

Dear Sylvestre,

Your letter was the cherry on top of this three-day weekend . . .
You are such a talented writer! And I love how you are trying to
manipulate me! How could I refuse reading your manuscript when
you've opened your heart to me?

I can confirm what you already know: I am impatiently waiting
for the new end of your novel and I'm dying to know what outcome you'll choose. Will you follow the dreams that you clung to
at the time, or remain faithful to reality? Don't tell me anything . . .
I'll quietly wait for you to conquer your demons and for your pen
alone to decide the outcome.

In the meantime, I'd like to learn more about your life. What
do you do for a living and how do you have so much free time if
you have not yet reached the age of retirement (which, you have
noticed, retreats gradually as we approach it, like a carrot dangled
in front of a donkey in an attempt to keep it moving)?

As for me, I never stop running around, like your wife, even if
my destinations are less recreational: office, work meetings, super-
markets to supply the household, school visits for the higher-level

education of my children, and so on and so forth . . . Give me something to look forward to and tell me when I can finally experience the joy of theater clubs, gymnastics classes, meals at a restaurant, and especially time to relax in the middle of the week! Unless of course you are the descendant of a multimillionaire family, in which case this will never be an option for me.

And no, I won't explain to you what I meant about the female behaviors you probably misinterpreted thirty years ago. Holding no degree in female psychology, my only knowledge comes from my age and the fact that I am a woman. I will only say that I am amazed that you were so naïve that you believed that a young woman is not in love simply because she does not say that she is . . . Why insist on the honesty and transparency of the "weaker" sex when it is not possessed by those of the supposedly stronger sex?

One last thing: How can you remain impartial about the journey taken by your book? You lost it more than thirty years ago between two airports, I found it at the end of the world (for the Bretons, that goes without saying) and you're not at all curious to know how it got there?

You have to admit that it's rather unbelievable that these pages could travel all these years on the wind and tides without anyone throwing them in the recycling bin. Not that I think your book doesn't deserve to survive, but our fellow citizens normally demonstrate a certain negligence with things that don't belong to them . . .

You probably think I'm overstepping, but I admit to a typically feminine curiosity concerning this mystery. With my network of

Breton relations, I have set in motion a plan that, I hope, will allow us to identify the author of the last pages and to find out how your book arrived in Finistère . . .

Your indiscreet correspondent,

Anne-Lise

from Sylvestre to Anne-Lise

LES CHAYETS, MAY 18, 2016

Does my book really deserve so much fuss? I am astonished at the idea of all these Breton souls trying to find my coauthor . . . I hadn't considered the possibility of meeting him one day and I'm amazed to find that you are ready to smoke him out and make him admit to writing something he might not wish to take responsibility for.

It's true that my nature is to be private—my friends would say secretive—and that I have a tendency to be reserved around all people I spend time with. I would never have dared, for example, to ask you questions about your hobbies and your profession as you asked me with such ease. To answer you, I'll simply say that I am not yet retired, and also not the rich descendant of a wealthy family free from material concerns. No. I am merely lucky enough to be able to work from home, with access to a computer and an Internet connection.

If it seems I spend my days being lazy, it's because I only sleep four hours at night and I abuse my keyboard while my colleagues rest their neurons. It's so I can take advantage of the best hours of the day to stroll or lounge in an armchair with a book in my hand.

But don't worry, you're not writing to a freeloader, I diligently fulfill the professional duties I am assigned . . .

I don't know whether the frantic rhythm that guides your existence suits you (in which case you would belong, like my wife, to the category of Rodents, a name I've chosen because they always seem to be running after something that they alone can see) or if you are the opposite, and you aspire to a more contemplative life and see business as a necessary evil (which would classify you, like me, in the category of Folivora . . .).

I hope the weekend you spent on the shore of the Iroise Sea at least allowed you to clear your head. Have you noticed the tyranny we typically exert on our minds? When we order our thoughts to follow a straight path that's already been drawn rather than allowing it to deviate as it should?

Try this experiment: isolate yourself from your peers (for example one day when your family is going to a hockey game or a costume ball or any other type of activity, fake a horrible headache that will force you to stay home alone), sit at a window that looks out onto a patch of greenery or, if you are hopelessly surrounded by concrete, choose a tree spurting out of a sidewalk. Sit however you wish, in a chaise longue, cross-legged on a piece of furniture, with your back against your balcony wall, it doesn't matter, and observe. Begin by contemplating the trunk as if it were the magnificent accomplishment of a great and little-known sculptor, then, slowly, let your eyes climb along the branches until you reach the highest twig you can make out.

Why? When I do this exercise, my mind surrenders completely. I hope that you will also feel that lightness of being—a state in which nothing is dictated.

I'll stop this flight of fancy here because I don't want you to take me for a Buddhist or an expert of any other form of spirituality, which is not the case. I simply crossed paths with a vocational rehabilitation advisor and those people have a certain talent for distracting our attention from the elements that disturb it . . .

Sylvestre

from Anne-Lise to Sylvestre

Dear Sylvestre,

Has my curiosity unsettled you? It's true that as I grow older, I prefer to take the more direct path, in life and in conversation. If you had known me at twenty years old, you would have been amazed by my silence and my restraint, and of course, I would have never bothered you by asking about your life or conducting research on your book without your consent.

Now that the harm is done, I owe you the details that I now know. The plot thickens around your manuscript and soon we will require the help of a real Hercule Poirot to resolve what I will call henceforth "the mystery of room 128" . . .

I have a dear friend, Maggy, who lives year-round in the small Breton port where I spent that infamous weekend in April. Thanks to our long friendship and a natural tendency to drag each other into incredible adventures since the age of ten, she agreed to go to the hotel to find out who had left your novel in the spot where I'd found it (here I am acting like the owner when I only stayed there three nights). After an interview with the staff, we have concluded that the object in question (the term doesn't do you justice, but it shows you just how much the investigators have entered into their roles) was introduced into room 128 two days before my arrival. I won't go into the details but, bizarrely, I think we will have to expand our search to all the occupants of the hotel.

Why, you will ask. I don't know yet. However, refusing on principle to give up, I came up with a plan likely to get us past this roadblock (perhaps this "us" is a bit presumptuous? If that's the case, I promise to put a stop to the whole thing).

I wrote a letter that was sent, with the permission of the hotel manager, to all the people who stayed in the hotel on the date in question.

Dear Sir (Madam),

You stayed at the Beau Rivage Hotel on . . . and we hope that you have a pleasant memory of your stay. In order to assist a guest, we are hoping to find the origin of a manuscript forgotten in one of the rooms of our establishment. If you have the slightest clue to help us figure out where it came from, we would appreciate it if you could please contact the person at the address below.

We thank you in advance for any information you can give us, no matter how seemingly trivial, and we hope to welcome you very soon for another stay at the Beau Rivage Hotel.

Blah blah blah.

Here, dear Sylvestre, is the template I sent to my friend. I have little hope of receiving a response, but at least I will know that I have tried everything to discover the identity of your coauthor.

Hoping for your support for my plan.

Your Belgian detective (minus the mustache!),

Anne-Lise

P.S. How did you know that I detest costume parties and sporting events? I don't remember sharing these details and I am surprised by how well you know me already . . . Am I that obvious?

P.P.S. I belong to the category of Folivora, even if I had to look up what this curious animal is . . .

from Nahima Reza to Anne-Lise Briard

RUE MAURICE-THOREZ, SAINT-DENIS, MAY 22, 2016

Madame Briard,

I'm writing to you following the letter addressed to me by the manager of the Beau Rivage Hotel in Le Conquet. The letter mentioned a manuscript and I know how it arrived in her establishment. I'm the one who put it there, and I left it in room 128 because August 12 (the twelfth day of the eighth month), is an important date for me.

I don't know what connection you have to this book, but for you to contact all the clients of the hotel, as you've done, it must hold a lot of value to you. Is it yours? Do you know the author?

I picked it up on the beach in Roscoff on January 17. Flipping through it, I quickly understood that I was holding the original copy and therefore that it was missing from its owner. So I brought it to the bartender of the Bellevue, who was manning the heated terrace nearby. He thanked me, then confessed that he was the one who had placed the novel on the beach, in the hopes of a walker picking it up. I must have been what he had in mind because he suggested I keep it. Apparently it had transformed his life. So I read it.

Five times. Yes, it took a little while for the words to imprint themselves onto my mind and eventually into my body. Two weeks later, I sat in front of a mirror to do my makeup. Nothing out of the ordinary for you, probably. But I had spent months wallowing in front of the TV in a shapeless tracksuit, eating cakes and watching trash TV, and that sudden interest in my appearance was something of a miracle. Over the following days, the transformation continued. I returned to the Paris area. I went to the office and all my colleagues saw me reborn. At night, I plunged back into this book that I kept on the coffee table next to my couch and, little by little, the weight that I had been dragging around seemed lighter. Until the day when I decided to get in touch with my child. I don't know you well enough to tell you about my past, and we would need more of a relationship for me to tell you about all this.

You must be asking yourself why I abandoned the book in that hotel. The answer is simple. When I met my son for the first time, I was staying there. I thought of that bartender who had saved me and I wanted to show the same generosity. I decided the guesthouse on the cul-de-sac facing the sea was a good choice, for I believe it's the kind of place we visit when we have to make a decision that will determine the rest of our lives. This manuscript had already proven its worth twice over and I wanted to give it the chance to help a third reader.

There you have it, now you know everything, or close to it.

Cordially,

Nahima Reza

from Anne-Lise to Sylvestre

RUE DES MORILLONS, MAY 25, 2016

Dear Sylvestre,

Bingo! I've found the person who left your book in room 128! It was a young woman who owes a lot to your words. The glimpse of life outlined in her letter profoundly moved me and I'm sure it will have the same effect on you.

I'm attaching a copy of her letter for you here.

Warmly,

Anne-Lise

P.S. Do you think you will pitch your story to a publisher once you finish it? Is it really autobiographical? And if so, have you spoken of that part of your life to those who share it today?

P.P.S. I am annoyingly curious so feel free to ignore the above questions without any hard feelings.

From Anne-Lise to Nahima

Dear Nahima,

I'm addressing you by your first name and I hope you won't be offended. You don't know me, I know nothing about you, or almost nothing, and yet, I feel as though we share a big secret. We've both read a novel that should never have fallen into our hands, an intimate and delicate work that was not meant for us, but which shook up our existences.

I am not personally involved in this work. I am merely a book lover and this book moved me. I wanted to meet its author, or rather its authors, because it was written by four hands. Of course, there is love in these pages. But above all there is that cliffhanger ending to the story . . .

Perhaps it's that mystery that buries its teeth in us once the book is finished. It's certainly that suspense that gives the book a timeless and incomplete quality.

I will now approach, via a proxy, the bartender who gave you this beautiful gift. My journey continues and, who knows, perhaps that man will guide me to another reader.

I cannot end this letter without mentioning my wish to hear

more about your child (and yet, I swore that I would restrain my-self). I just wonder how this novel led you to him (God knows that "just" is an understatement!). But you are speaking to someone who isn't shy, as you are well aware now that you've seen what I'm capable of doing for a simple manuscript. You don't have to answer me, unless you'd like to, and no matter what, I thank you with all my heart for having sent me your first letter.

Sending a hug to you and to your child as well,

Anne-Lise

P.S. Did you choose the Beau Rivage Hotel because it's all the way at the very tip of the country? And do you really believe that bringing oneself to the end of the road helps to open other doors?

from Sylvestre to Anne-Lise

It's true, I was a bit annoyed with you for entering into my life without knocking and leading a search that should have been my own. But your last letter erased all resentment. Nahima's words flooded my daily life like one of those catchy tunes that have the inexplicable power of bringing us out of our sadness despite ourselves. Thank you for contacting her. Thank you for sharing all the good she got out of the book.

Is this what sustains writers and gives them the strength to confront the blank page? The certainty that in the end, they'll be able to save someone from despair? My mood is as stable as a dead leaf drifting in an Autan wind. On the one hand, the joy of feeling that power; on the other, the regret at not having seized that opportunity on a larger scale by publishing the book and multiplying by ten or a hundred the happiness that I've just discovered.

I will satisfy your curiosity even though I don't have to. No, my wife doesn't know about the existence of this manuscript, and neither does my daughter. Yes, the brief romance that spans those pages is autobiographical. And no, for those two reasons, I don't envision submitting the book to a publisher, who, in any event, would send it back to me at the first opportunity. I am certainly naïve, but not enough to believe that a narrative that contains no shouts, no revolt, not an ounce of the supernatural, and no trace of a political message can pique the interest of a scrutinizing editor on the hunt for a bestseller . . . And then, the idea of revealing, at fifty-six years old, to those around me that I've kept in the back of my mind the memory of a bygone romance would start conversations I wouldn't want to bring about for anything in the world.

You have fulfilled your mission of finding the person who brought my book to the tip of Brittany. Now you can turn to other projects. I have to say that I've taken a liking to our exchanges, which have allowed me to meet my mailman. In fact, no one writes to me anymore and all my bills now arrive electronically. With the "no junk mail" sticker my daughter put on the letterbox after a tenth-grade exposé on deforestation, I thought of doing away with that obsolete object altogether . . . Thanks to you, it's regained its utility for a bit.

And you should know: you have reawakened the fervor for writing in me. Not only am I now determined to finish my old novel, but I am embarking simultaneously on a new book that keeps me up until the middle of the night.

So you can be happy knowing you've saved an idle fifty-something from his ennui.

Sylvestre

POINTE DES RENARDS, MAY 29, 2016

Hi Lisou!

Who else but you could lead me down such unbelievable paths?
And is there any other friend I would set out for to taste the wind of
the North (yes, yes, for me, Roscoff is the North) while the spring
sun is warming up the plants on my patio? It's a fact that you alone
have this power to get me on the road even when the amateur pho-
tographers have refused to go to Finistère, frustrated by the fuel
shortage that has us gathered in front of gas stations like junkies
harassing their dealers . . .

It's even worse that I was not satisfied by merely obeying the
request you made over the phone (on that note, you can thank Agathe for relaying your requests so valiantly), but I did so with an
incredible excitement. Upon arriving in Roscoff at noon, I went
to the Bellevue and made no mention of my reason for being there
before I had tasted their scallops roasted in butter (don't forget that
you're paying, I made sure to keep the receipt), along with a glass
of 2005 Gros Plant, a very good year chosen with the help of the
server (who it so happens was very cute).

I took advantage of a lull in the service (I don't understand why restaurant owners complain when their places are filled to the brim a month before the official close for paid vacation!) to question Roméo (I swear that's his name). I had barely mentioned the manuscript on the beach when he asked if I wanted to have coffee during his break (I have to mention here that I still have a perfect tan from my vacation and that I was wearing my little floral dress, even though my teeth chattered with each gust of wind!). Our Roméo, who owes his name to his Italian mother, found the manuscript at the Roscoff library, where he hosts workshops for schoolchildren. This waiter is a literature enthusiast and goes to the library whenever he has time.

To temper this idyllic description of a perfect young man, you should know that he started to frequent the library because he was infatuated by a young librarian . . . But at the end of the day, don't you always say that we are driven to read for the best reasons?

One winter day, he was watching his ladylove while volunteering for a neighborhood association when a man came to the counter with a collection of books he wanted to donate to the library. It was all the way at the bottom of a box, beneath dozens of dog-eared and yellowed books, that our Roméo found this manuscript that now occupies all my thoughts even though I have yet to read it.

Our charming young man learned from it that unconfessed love can stay with us an entire lifetime, and so he decided to get over his shyness and declare his feelings for the young librarian named Julie (I swear to you that this is all true and that Julie is her real name) . . . They're not married and don't have children, but I think it's only because they haven't had enough time, and I dare to hope that "Roméo" and "Julie" will conquer the tragedy of their namesakes to live happily for years to come!

Now you know everything, my dear Lisou, and thanks to you I spent a magnificent day in Roscoff, which is, by the way, a town well worth the trek . . .

I would have loved to make you languish—to use an expression that couldn't be any less Breton—but I am your friend and I was too afraid you'd get worked up all alone and get one of your ulcers again. So yes, I asked THE question: Is there any way to find the man who donated the box?

Roméo doesn't know his name, but he's going to ask around and will contact you as soon as he knows more. I gave him your information (I'm handing him over to you only because he's too young for me, but I assure you he's very cute and no, I don't doubt the power of my floral dress).

What do you think? Haven't I played a good Watson?

I know I've made you proud and that as you read these words you have that brilliant smile on your face that urges your friends to do impossible and sometimes reprehensible acts in your name.

But I regret nothing, you have awakened in me the excitement that allows us to relive the adventures of our childhood heroes and I remain available for all investigations being conducted in my area.

Now I have to get back to work (I'm behind because of my little escapade) and I hope the rest of your weekend will be brightened up by these revelations.

Your adoring Watson,

Maggy

P.S. You know what? The handsome Roméo was wearing a red-and-white-striped T-shirt, and with his glasses, he reminded me of Waldo. You know *Where's Waldo?*, that series of books where the reader has to find a character in a striped T-shirt and a red hat in every image? It struck me that that's exactly what you're doing with your second author: you turn the pages and in each new setting, you search for your Waldo!

P.P.S. I just read an article on the puffer fish. It has a big head, bulging eyes, and a small, slippery body. Throw in some stretchy skin that allows it to puff up to repel predators, and a poison in its flesh that's deadly to man, and you will have a very accurate portrait of someone you know. Wouldn't that make an excellent pet for Bastien?

from Anne-Lise to Maggy

RUE DES MORILLONS, JUNE 2, 2016

Dear Maggy,

You are the best friend anyone could ask for! I can't wait to share the latest progress with you. Your young waiter called the man with the box and gave him my number (he apologized in a little message; you were right, he's a charming boy). I've just received a call from the man, a certain Mr. Cléder who lives in the western suburbs of Paris. Since he works very close to here, we're going to have lunch together tomorrow afternoon.

I'm beginning to think, Maggy, that this manuscript has the power to lower our defenses. Since its appearance in room 128, we have retraced the steps of its readers and, each time we mention it, doors open and faces light up.

Do you remember the long conversations we had about this thirty years ago? At university, we searched for "The Book." We dreamed of a text that would divert the anger of wounded hearts, that would shatter the hatred we feel for the unknown, chase away the clouds that leave premature wrinkles on still-young faces, a text that could provoke unbelievable and unforgettable encounters between people.

Don't roll your eyes! I abandoned that utopian vision more than thirty years ago, but when I write to people who've read Sylvestre's book, I rediscover my passion for reading and I believe in the power of words again.

There, I've said it. Your mocking tone won't change anything— this novel does its readers good and I promise to send you a copy. You know me, I couldn't keep myself from scanning the original before sending it back to its owner. (Of course, you'd have it faster if you joined our modern world and accepted the Internet into your lair.) In the meantime, I'm dying to meet this Mr. Cléder, who could very well be my "Waldo"!

I'll keep you posted.

Kisses,

Lisou

P.S. Having two managers for the same company should be banned, especially when the managers are related by blood. This morning, Bastien used our weekly meeting to put down my work once again. I said nothing. I flashed him my best smile. That reaction glued his mouth shut more effectively than all the responses I usually throw his way! It's because this "quest" gives me a sort of legitimacy that extends even to the office . . . but all the same I jotted down the name of that poison because, two streets over, there's a Japanese restaurant owner who owes me a favor . . .

from Anne-Lise to Sylvestre

RUE DES MORILLONS, JUNE 5, 2016

Dear Sylvestre,

It's not over yet! You thought I was going to stop at the Breton border? Well then you don't know me at all, because my path continues in Waldo's footsteps (no, I don't have his first name yet; that's a reference from my friend Maggy to a childhood cartoon by Martin Handford. Children have to find a small character with a striped sweater in the middle of a multicolored crowd, and I plan to find our man before the last page). I get more excited every day. I talk about my progress all the time at home, and without batting an eye I tolerate the mocking winks Julian (my partner) and the children give each other. How could I expect them to understand my passion for literature? They think that we forget to live our own lives when we slide into the existence of others . . .

As you may have guessed, when we are all at the table they generally half-listen to me and they find it amusing to indulge my pastime of choice. Nevertheless, yesterday, all three stopped chewing in unison when I announced my trip to Brussels (more on that later), and Julian shook his head while rolling his eyes (which

51

brought about a coughing fit because his mouth was full . . . nicely done!).

For nearly two months now, I've had a small place in the back of my mind for your book and for the very particular impact it has had on the people whose paths it has crossed. I suspect my husband thinks that I'm exaggerating. He's always known my love for books but complains that they invade my daily life. As soon as he sees the dreamy look on my face when an author infects my mind, he reacts as if he had come upon a lover hidden in our bedroom closet. I even hear him sigh when I slide with delight into our bed and throw myself without restraint at one of the numerous novels piled up on my nightstand. So of course, the idea of this trip to a village with an unpronounceable name whose official language is Dutch doesn't make him happy at all.

To explain to you (finally) why I'm going over there, I have to tell you about the man who left your novel at Roscoff. I met him on Friday. He's named Victor Cléder and he's in charge of an office of European affairs. Don't ask me what his job is; I wasn't listening to his explanation, I was too impatient for him to get to the reason for our meeting.

I only know that he lives between Paris and Brussels and develops business relations in both places. When he's in Belgium, he stays in Huldenberg, in a studio he rents from a couple of friends. It was there, accompanying their son to his weekly sports practice, that Victor discovered your manuscript. He's not a sports fanatic and was glad to kill the time with this novel abandoned on a chair.

At the end of the practice, he decided to bring it back to Paris so he could read the end, without even stopping to wonder whether it belonged to someone. He still had a few dozen pages left to read when he went to Roscoff to sort out his grandmother's will (either our friend is a slow reader, or he's overworked and only picks up the book three times per month).

What do you think he does once he's finished the book? Go on, guess . . . Victor decides to switch careers! He swears that this little revolt had been planned for a long time . . . That might be true, but it wasn't until after reading your book that he decided to stop his incessant back-and-forth between the European authorities that employ him! In six months, he will say good-bye to the various offices to take a sabbatical year.

Keep in mind that Victor is not a big reader and certainly not a man to change his beliefs because of a book. He also started to squander away his Breton inheritance by getting rid of all his family's books, and I would have openly declared him "boorish" if he hadn't had information for me. He doesn't even remember sliding your book to the bottom of one of those boxes and I think we can write off his gesture as a simple mistake. But we know (at least I do) that without the discovery of your book, he would still be a busy man, torn between his dreams and his job for a few more years . . .

So here I am ready to face your Belgian readers to find our Waldo. Don't be mad at me . . . I simply can't give up when we're so close to our goal.

Warmly,

Anne-Lise

P.S. I hope that the flooding going on not far from you won't affect your mailman's route . . . Perhaps his tenacity will spur him to complete his mission aboard a canoe!

from Sylvestre to Anne-Lise

What are you playing at?

Reading your first letter, I thought you lived the hectic and very full life of a woman with a demanding profession (you spoke of late meetings) all while raising two teenagers and managing the household. Yet here you are on the point of neglecting family and work to go off and chase a stranger, the author of the end of a book that has nothing to do with you!

Why try to pursue him thirty years later? Are you aware that your Waldo doesn't care at all about this book? Or did the second half of the book impress you so much that you hope to come upon an established, famous writer? Are you nothing but a groupie in the end, collecting autographs and selfies?

Sorry! I'm attacking you again. I have a tendency to neglect all manners now that I've retreated to the countryside where my few interlocutors are the moles in the garden and the spiders in the attic. You relayed the sentiments of my readers and I thank you for that, because it has evoked in me an unexpected and overwhelming emotion. But the thought of a search that leads you to abandon those around you in addition to your work to go to the four corners of the globe?

Stop this senseless running around right now. Once I've conquered my fear of travel, I promise I'll visit Brussels and pick back up the trail where you left off. It's an enticing city and now you've given me additional motivation to go. But don't get in trouble with your loved ones for a few old pages from thirty years ago, that would be ridiculous. Or, if you have a real reason to set out on the hunt for this Waldo, explain it to me and don't leave me hanging, worried I'll soon hear you've been committed because of me.

I await your response.

Sylvestre

P.S. My response serves as proof that the mailman is still making his way through our streets. He's wearing a raincoat and boots, but the showers haven't discouraged him. I believe he thinks highly of his job, and would finish his route by boat if the bad weather persists . . .

from Anne-Lise to Maggy

RUE DES PIERRES, BRUSSELS, JUNE 11, 2016

Dear Maggy,

Do you remember how we dreamed of visiting Brussels a few years ago? Well, let's get back to planning again, please, because this city is magnificent. You can't resist the charm of the Grand Place with all its shops overflowing with souvenirs and chocolate . . . When we were young, we would always bring back the kitschiest gifts for our friends and I'm sure we could break a record if we resumed our game here! On that note, I bought a little present that will brilliantly decorate the shelf of your living room . . .

Tonight I'm writing to you from the hotel I booked for two nights near the chocolate museum . . . It's adorable and I've eaten very well here during this short trip. I have the window half open; a slight breeze rustles the curtains and I can hear snippets of conversations from the street. As I write this letter, I'm appreciating the tidbits of anonymous lives that are invading my subconscious.

I am alone. How long has it been since I was last alone? We forget ourselves so much by looking at others, getting to know them, trying to exist in their eyes, that when they're far away, we no longer know who we are. So I'm thinking of your life in voluntary exile and I envy you a bit.

Tomorrow I'll return to Paris, after a mandatory trip to the Jacques Brel museum. We'll see the other sites together as soon as you're able to come back with me. I'll leave the children with their father, just this once won't hurt, and they're old enough to cook some pasta, aren't they? Speaking of which, I revel in my weekend even more when I think of Julian taking care of the groceries, the meals, and responding (with a smile) to all the demands of our two needy teenagers . . . Does that make me a bad mother?

I know you're waiting to hear an update. Donning my detective cap, I went to the neighborhood of Huldenberg as soon as I arrived to visit its famous soccer club. There I met an adorable old woman who could speak to me in French (though at first I thought she was speaking to me in Dutch, her accent was so strong). Eventually I got used to it and we drank tea together in her little house right next to the soccer field. In exchange for this lodging provided by the city, she looks after the area and monitors the comings and goings between games.

In order to convince her to help me out, I told her the entire story of this manuscript (the more I tell it, the more extraordinary I find it!). She listened to me attentively, sipping her tea. Then, eyes shining, she told me that my search wouldn't stop at her door and that she would help find the man (or woman) who had left the book in her locker rooms. Since good fortune has accompanied me on each step of this journey, I wasn't surprised to learn there would be a game the next day and that all the regulars were expected to attend.

So, at the end of the afternoon, I returned to the home of Hanne Janssen (that's her name). She was accompanied by a teenager with a grumpy expression that I know by heart since I see it every day on my Katia's face. The young girl was sulking, for this novel had resulted in her being grounded for two weeks. Her mother had asked her to return it to her best friend, an old Parisian woman who wanted to read it and must have also told her how to get to the address on page 156 from Paris. Of course, the young girl forgot it on the locker room bench and it disappeared.

Since her mother is currently completing an internship in our capital (talk about coincidence), we agreed to meet before her return to Brussels, two weeks from now. I am so excited . . . No, I am going to be honest, I am hopping up and down with impatience at the idea of this next meeting!

So to help me endure the wait, I've collected a mountain of information on all the sites we can visit during our next trip to the Belgian capital . . .

Figure out your dates, we'll organize our escapade as soon as I get back.

Kisses,

Lisou

from Ellen Anthon to Anne-Lise Briard

GARE DU NORD, PARIS, JUNE 15, 2016

Dear Madame Briard,

I'm so sad that I'm not able to meet you in Paris as we had agreed! Unfortunately, I was told this afternoon that my husband has been hospitalized in Brussels with a hernia. It's not very serious and I know he's doing fine, but if you know men (I imagine French men are as bad as Belgian men when they're ill), you'll understand that he would take it the wrong way if I were to stay in Paris while he's dying in Brussels!

Since this book moved you as much as it moved me, I won't make you wait for an explanation on how it came into my possession. I'm going to call the friend who gave it to me and he'll tell you the whole story better than I could. In any event, I'm quite pleased to know that you found it and its owner. Tell him that his novel is impatiently awaited in Belgium and that it's never good to stumble *en stoemelings*.

There are twenty of us in my book club in Belgium and we all loved this story, which showed up right after we started our writing workshop. Our poetry leader is the one who brought it to us. I'll send him your information so he can tell you more because now I

61

need to get going. Fortunately for my dying husband, the 5:49 P.M. TGV is on time despite your legendary strikes . . .

At your service,

Ellen Anthon

P.S. I would be very happy to meet you if you come back *volle gas* to our country. I really enjoyed your city even though Parisians lack a sense of humor (except of course when they're making fun of my fellow citizens).

from William Grant to Anne-Lise Briard

GREAT PETER STREET, LONDON, JUNE 19, 2016

Madame Briard,

I am writing to you at the request of our mutual friend, Ellen Anthon. I learned that you are interested in a text that was in my possession only a few months ago. It doesn't belong to me and I don't know the identity of its author. But the story touched me, and I kept it with me for a while until I gave it up to my Bruxellois friends. My profession requires a lot of moving around; I am not the permanent leader of the association you heard about, but I quite like the people in it and I attend their meetings whenever I'm in Brussels.

Right now, I'm on a trip to London and I think I'll stay here for a little while because I have some family in the area. Since my mother is Franco-Belgian, I also had a French grandmother and, as a child, spent all my summers in the south of your beautiful country, where I still have a house. Please excuse the bragging: I am merely trying to explain that I am often in France. On my next visit, if you like, we can meet to talk about the book.

I added a few words on the last pages: lines that I left there as if the text were a collective composition inviting each reader to write

63

the next part . . . Thank you for apologizing to the owner on my behalf for having taken this liberty that was justified only by the pleasure of enjoying a nice moment thanks to his narrative talents.

With my best wishes,

William Grant

from Sylvestre to Anne-Lise

LES CHAYETS, JUNE 22, 2016

It's now been more than two weeks since I've heard from you. I assume from this that you have not taken my advice and that you went to Belgium against everyone's wishes. Did you think about me at all? Did you stop to think that it might be unpleasant for me to meet the man who finished my work and lent it an appeal that I did not manage to breathe into the first pages?

Yes, this morning I am angry, Anne-Lise, and I wonder whether I should burn this manuscript and put an end to your wanderings. I don't understand the motivation for your quest; we don't know each other, and this story is not yours!

You are not the only reason for my frustration: it's now June and this time of year always plunges me into a state of feverishness leading to bad decisions. I believe we all have an unfavorable month that we hold our breath through each year in order to fight back the noxiousness. Now you know mine. At least I have the good fortune that this month is only thirty days, which diminishes my period of aggravation by about three percent compared to half the population, but it's nearly seven percent longer for me than for those lucky few who loathe February!

And don't use my bad mood as an excuse to leave me in the dark. Own your indiscretion and at least keep me updated on your discoveries!

Sylvestre

P.S. I'll wait until July to burn my pages. That way I will not be able to attribute this decision to the bad influence of this cursed month. For a few days now, the heavy heat making its way from Paris to here only reinforces my irritation and the uninspired journalists bring out their usual refrains on the heat wave, as if this eight-letter phrase were their secret password to getting on the *20 Heures* news show. Is the weather the same in Belgium?

from Nahima to Anne-Lise

Hello Anne-Lise,

I've been waiting to answer you. I needed a little while to sort out my life and to try to find time for writing letters again. When I wrote to you, a month ago, I had just seen my child. That possessive is an exaggeration because I abandoned this child at birth. I was barely sixteen years old, but that's not an excuse; this fact doesn't change the gravity of my action.

I told my family a story about a high school boyfriend and a birthday party. I was so ashamed. Who could I tell that I had agreed to meet with my rapist? And anyway, I had forgotten everything. When I think about the assault now, it's as though it happened to someone else, or that someone told the story to me, or that I saw it on a reality TV show. I feel such detachment when faced with the horror of that moment that no one would have believed me if I had recounted the graffiti obscuring the gray of the walls, the color of the sky visible through the skylight, the stench of the trash and the odors of rotting fish that wafted through the half-open door. And how to superimpose on this vulgar scene the joyous soundtrack of the cries of carefree children playing in the town park? Even the blade of the knife that gashed my throat didn't leave any memory of pain. Just a small, bright red triangle under my jaw that I hid with a bit of foundation for a few days.

At fifteen years old, I repressed my rape so well that I saw none of the signs that should have alerted me. By the time I accepted the reality, it was too late. My parents were there, they supported me despite the disappointment they must have felt. They offered to help me raise my child. I refused.

The birth happened. And life went on. That's what I wanted. For everything to go back to how it was before. Live the same life as the other girls in the neighborhood again. Go out as a group. Avoid the town basements and confidently mock those girls who give in and refuse to wear skirts to high school. Assume the courage that only teenagers have, get back to the shores of unconsciousness . . .

But I hadn't understood that, in the meantime, I had become a mother. A child-mother, a mother without a child, call it what you will.

It all began with little things, a jump hearing a cry on the stairs, a violent pain in my stomach seeing advertisements featuring babies. I would cry more and more often, and my parents ended up calling the adoption service. Once again, it was too late. The child had been placed in a family, there was nothing to do. I started to analyze the faces of all the babies I saw. I became obsessed, to the extent that I paid someone to get the name of the adoptive family. He did. When my parents found out, they sent me to the therapist I had seen after the birth. He was the only one who knew the real circumstances of my pregnancy. He forbade me from going to see my child and advised me to put distance between us. I left to go to my aunt's, near Paris, thinking that a change of scenery would allow me to forget. It didn't work. For eight years, I dragged around that guilt and that "sentimental uncertainty." That's how my shrink referred to my unhappiness. But he was wrong, it wasn't a matter of sentimentality; I had left a part of me in a county hospital and I was moving forward, incomplete.

When I picked up that manuscript in Roscoff, I was on leave for depression and I was temporarily back living in my parents' house. Of course, the story in the book has nothing to do with mine, but it showed me to what extent our existence is insignificant. You might say it's a strange way to reawaken a lust for life! But it's not all that strange, because the more our passage on Earth is trivial and fleeting, the more the decisions we make become unimportant, almost forgivable . . .

In this state of mind, I reached out to my son. He's named Romain, he lives with a wonderful family and has two little sisters who adore him. His parents told him about his adoption and they allowed me to meet him on April 14. I saw him. And I finally discovered who I was. Perhaps it's obvious for you if you have children . . . but for me, that day changed everything. An unexpected, animal violence. From deep inside me, the force that can turn a mother into a saint or a criminal. I understood that, for the being standing in front of me, unaware of the love he provoked, I could now kill, or erase myself. I could remain in the shadows if I knew that that would allow him to be happy. And wait. For the smallest sign on his part.

I know now that his life will continue far from me, but they will let me see him each time he expresses the desire, his mother promised me that.

After that meeting in Brest, I remained in Finistère for a few days, in that hotel where I decided to reintegrate into the world of the living and give my life another chance. And that's why I placed those words that had sustained me for two months in room 128, where you found them.

That's the whole story. If you're now in contact with the people who wrote this novel, I would be happy to have their information. I believe they deserve to know the influence they've had on my life.

Affectionately,

Nahima

P.S. You said that we have both "read an intimate and delicate work that was not meant for us." Do you still believe that? I know that it was waiting for me and that it wound up on the beach that day so that I could regain my path and advance a bit further. Sometimes there is a clear connection between a book and a reader; it can't just be a coincidence.

from Maggy to Anne-Lise

VINCENT SQUARE, LONDON, JUNE 28, 2016

Hello Lisou!

I've arrived! You were right, London is magnificent! Yesterday, I walked until eleven P.M. on the banks of the Thames, I breathed in the sea air which caressed my face as if it had accompanied me here from home. Indifferent to the humid chill that enveloped us, there were dozens of us daydreaming on the shore of the gray, tormented water and I imagine that stroll has inspired more novels than all my coastal trails combined.

Despite my incapacity to understand what is being said around me (or more likely because of it), I feel at home here. Did you feel the same during your trips? It's a delicious and troubling sensation to feel like you belong in a place where you've never set foot . . .

This morning, I drifted along with the wind, which glides from one intersection to another as if to spread the fragrance of the river. I wandered down streets and smiled, capturing a few unknown words, which I had fun guessing the meaning of according to the speakers' facial expressions. Then, a ray of sun pierced the heart of the clouds. I settled in its light, on the edge of a terrace, and I observed the people passing by. I discovered England, my eyes amazed by the senseless outfit pairings, my sense of smell titillated by the pungent "fish and chips," and my hearing captivated by the unexpected sounds.

When it was time to eat, I contacted your Mr. Grant, who fortunately speaks French as well as I do (I promise to work on my English again as soon as I get back). He couldn't meet today, but suggested places to visit when he found out this was my first time in London. We agreed to meet for lunch tomorrow in a bistro.

Do you realize what you've asked me to do? I hate leaving my home, and yet, here I am in this city whose language I don't speak, initiating an encounter with a stranger who, you admit, you know nothing about! Are you aware he could be a descendent of Jack the Ripper? I could be risking my life for you!

I've got to get to sleep if I want to see all of your William's recommendations tomorrow.

Kisses and goodnight,

Maggy

P.S. I hope your Englishman is not passionate about international politics and planning to launch into a discussion about Brexit. I would then be obligated to say that I have no opinion on the matter to avoid annoying a man who might have precious clues for us . . .

Note my diplomacy!

from Anne-Lise to Maggy

My dear Maggy,

I just received your two letters mailed Thursday from the London airport . . . What happened over there? What did this William Grant do to you? Is it the city or the man who has bewitched you? Is my best friend really the author of these words?

As soon as I entered, my gaze was drawn to a man, alone, sitting at the back of the pub. He was looking outside, a slight smile on his lips as if he were dreaming of happy days gone by. His profile was at once soft and determined and I prayed with all my strength that this man was Mr. Grant. He had barely turned his head toward me before he stood up from his chair with a charming and entirely English stiffness. He took my coat and we discussed the sights I had seen in the city. I had to make a superhuman effort to avoid his gray eyes and I concentrated on the wall decorations in order to speak naturally, as if I regularly had lunch across from seductive men with irresistible stares.

Maggy, tell me you didn't keep his address or his telephone number, please! What will you gain by falling in love with an Anglo-Franco-Belgian who, to top it off, occupies his time by playing poker? I am sorry for having sent you over there on a whim without doing any research into this man. Obviously he's a rogue who spends his time seducing women and gambling in casinos! At least I am reassured to know that despite the day you two spent together, you were able to get on a plane that carried you away from this seducer and back to your village, where you will forget this senseless adventure. And drop that silly idea of learning English; it's a dangerous language. Instead turn your attention to Brittany and find yourself a kind sailor who spends his time at sea and allows you to enjoy the liberty and solitude you went looking for in Finistère.

Nevertheless, that unwise escapade was not in vain, since now we know that after finding Sylvestre's manuscript at his parents' house, William Grant kept it for ten years. But with his father dead and his mother suffering from Alzheimer's, who can tell us how those pages arrived in Lozère?

It's strange that I have tears in my eyes at the idea that everything might end here and I thank heaven Julian isn't at home, because I might make another scene. This quest has taken too much space in my existence, I know, but that has nothing to do with what happened to me eight years ago. At the time, you remember, I had just lost my mother, and the emotional affair I threw myself into was nothing but a desperate act, an attempt to restart the beatings of my heart like a cardiac electroshock. That jerk wasn't important to me, and besides, his writing was rather mediocre. You understand that, so explain to me why Julian looks at me with distrust when I come home an hour late. I thought all that was far behind us and that we were past the age of conjugal suspicion.

With Sylvestre, my curiosity is purely literary. I can't stop myself from thinking that his novel is something special. Is it the fact that it was written by two authors who don't know each other? Is it the simplicity of the story that hangs in suspense, those naïve remarks or formulas for simple happiness created by a twenty-year-old man? I don't know, Maggy, but I have rediscovered the wonder of walking through my own city, the bus driver's smile at the end of the day, the smell of grass in the early morning when I cross through the Parc Georges-Brassens . . .

And now, should I share with Sylvestre the impasse we've found ourselves in?

Kisses,

Lisou

P.S. Forgive me once again for sending you on that crazy expedition to London. Forget that bewitching city and focus on our escape to Brussels . . . I promise, over there we'll avoid all gray eyes . . .

RUE DES MORILLONS, JULY 3, 2016

Dear Sylvestre,

Note that I waited for July to respond to you. I've been scolded enough on the subject of this book, whether by you or by members of my family. But you can mark this date as when you recovered your property and we put an end to the question "Where's Waldo?"

Candor is one of my qualities, and I assure you that my decision has nothing to do with your anger. Also nothing to do with any weariness on my part (perseverance is another of my character traits). To catch you up to speed, it was an Englishman, William Grant, who brought your book to Belgium and added a few lines to it. So I sent my friend Maggy to visit London and thank God she returned unscathed (well, almost). She met the man who kept your manuscript for years after finding it in his mother's belongings in 2006. Unfortunately, the poor thing is no longer in her right mind, and so we're having a hard time learning any more details about how it came into her possession.

It's true that my passion for your manuscript worries those around me. My husband and children are afraid that I have become enamored with an author and that I am guiltily concealing my infatuation behind a façade of literary interest. So I will not set out to challenge the memory loss of a woman afflicted with Alzheimer's and instead I'll give you the telephone number of her son if you wish to try your luck. Your turn to justify such a trip if you've still said nothing to your family . . .

That's where we're at, dear Sylvestre, and in case our exchanges start to taper off, I thank you in advance on my behalf and on behalf of all your readers for this beautiful story you have given us to read and for the resulting benefit it has brought to our lives. You have written a text that's spanned time and spread fragments of happiness all around it. It has brought about encounters and transformations in people's lives as only great masterpieces can do.

With all my gratitude and best wishes,

Anne-Lise

P.S. I can't keep the contact information of all the people who've helped me these last two months to myself. They've all read your work. So I'm including their addresses in case one day you'd like to correspond with them, which would bring you, I hope, as much satisfaction as it did me.

from William to Anne-Lise

Dear Madame Briard,

Despite what I had planned, I cannot come to Paris in the coming weeks. I beg your pardon, but I've been invited to Finistère, where I've never been, and suddenly this discovery feels urgent to me.

Nevertheless, I want you to know that I will go to Lozère next. Once there I will track down the clues that escaped me ten years ago when I found your friend's manuscript. During my previous attempts to sort through the family house, I kept falling on memories that stalled my progress. You see, each object seems to possess the power of recalling a multitude of lost images, as if it had preciously guarded the memory, which is returned to us when we hold the object in our hands. So I've put off sorting through the attic, the cellar, and my mother's former office.

This time, I am up to the challenge and have resolved to find new pieces of information that can help your search.

I will be sure to let you know before my next trip to Paris, and I hope we will have the opportunity to meet then.

Faithfully yours,

William Grant

GREAT PETER STREET, JULY 7, 2016

Hello dear Maggy!

Remember me? Say yes, because I took your invitation very seriously.

Before going to see my Belgian friends, I was supposed to stop in Paris, but your enthusiasm has convinced me that I simply cannot die without first seeing Finistère (not that I have a date with the Grim Reaper, but I'm the type to never delay the discovery of exotic lands).

So I will be in Brest the day after tomorrow at 2:15 P.M. Now that I've made my decision, I won't cancel this trip, no matter whether or not you want to see me. So you have a few options: you can be busy, in which case I will explore your region on my own; you can take back your invitation, and I will act in the same way without bothering you any further; but it's also possible that you have nothing better to do than guide a near-stranger through the Breton coast. If that is my luck, I'll wait for you until four P.M. at the Brest airport.

I estimate that you will receive this letter the day of my arrival; this is intentional. You will have only a few hours to make your decision, and it's often when we're in a hurry that we make the best choices. I typically live my life according to rolls of the dice, even if my specialty is poker. Since I started acting this way, things have become much simpler and I've never had a reason to regret it.

Hoping that luck will be on my side once again,

XXX

William

from Sylvestre to Anne-Lise

LES CHAYETS, JULY 8, 2016

I shouldn't have written you in June. Throw out my last letter. The regular reports you've sent me have brightened up my nights. For the past few months, I've started to write again, first sporadically, then more and more often, until I felt this pressing need to let go of what had been trapped within me for so many years. I abandoned my old manuscript for a new one which is not at all biographical, or only slightly. All of this I owe to you, and I don't take that lightly.

If I had known in 2006 that my book would rest some time in an attic in Lozère, that it would soon find its readers, stay with them, and sometimes comfort them, no doubt these last ten years would have been different . . .

When you're twenty years old, life seems welcoming, and though we suspect we will have obstacles to overcome, we believe we are ready to confront the assaults of oceans, the sand carried through the sky, and the relentless fury of the big cities. Three decades later, the path seems less straightforward. The summer storms have left behind ruts that make progress difficult. So we look back and tell ourselves that we were ill-prepared, that our ancestors saddled our genes with a weakness that others don't possess. We tell ourselves we were born too late, or too early. That the problems we face were planned or else that we missed a badly marked intersection. We tell ourselves above all that airports and train stations have stolen more from us than a few typewritten sheets of paper. But who cares! Today, I look back on my missteps with a peaceful gaze and I observe my novel's journey as one amuses themselves opening a Russian doll. Each layer reveals a new person hiding another within themselves.

So I thank this mysterious Waldo and I try to imagine him finding my property on the seat of an airplane and carrying it preciously home with him. The ending he invented has nothing to do with the one I would have chosen, but I think it lends more value to the story. If you are not too disappointed by my ungratefulness and we remain in contact despite everything, I will soon call on your experienced reader's opinion. Will you grant my request or have you crossed me off the list of your epistolary relations?

I understand the worry of those close to you, and I apologize. Reassure them as much as you can, slander my image and the opinion you have of me; all will be justified in the name of preserving your family. Just don't condemn our friendly correspondence . . .

Keep in mind that I am not the only one waiting for your response. If you stop our exchanges here, you will force the mailman to modify his route; currently he benefits from passing by my faded letterbox, which allows him to open my gate, cross my land, and take a private path which he doesn't normally have access to . . . This way he gains precious minutes on his route and the path is much less hilly than if he were to take the public roads. Take into consideration these unexpected implications of an abrupt stop to your letters.

I hope you're enjoying the beginning of summer,

Sylvestre

P.S. Thank you for taking the time to write to me in July when you, like most of our fellow citizens, must be preparing for your next vacation in the sun. Now we're in for six weeks of televised reports on the joys of paid vacation and the easy journey of the luckiest among us: their trips on the highway in single file (what happened to the Bison Futé travel information services of our youth?), their arrival at a camping ground on the Mediterranean coast, their meals on a terrace with a view of the path leading to the toilets, and finally the shots of their love handles on the greasy sand of a packed and noisy beach.

POINTE DES RENARDS, JULY 9, 2016

Dear Lisou,

I received the copy of the infamous manuscript. With all you told me about it, I have to admit that it disappointed me. I expected to have my breath taken away, to shake along with the protagonists, to ignore sleep in order to arrive at the conclusion more quickly . . . and I didn't feel that way at all. The story is so common that I wondered why you were so enchanted with it.

It wasn't until the middle of the following night that the words started to take effect and I understood. Once we've reached the last page, we feel more vulnerable to beauty. We look at the people we pass with an unusual benevolence, and that indulgence extends to our own reflection. I understand that this story helps us to smile and to put into perspective those trivial things that have the power to weigh on our days. In any case that's how I felt this morning when I got up, and curiously, at that very moment, I received a troubling letter. I won't tell you any more about it, my Lisou, but know that I have to make a decision in the next few hours and the idea makes me nervous. No matter what, when you read this, the decision will be behind me, and its implications too. So it's useless for me to make a list of the drawbacks to following up—or not—on the demand in question.

Don't worry, I'll tell you everything in more detail in a few days. Now I have to get going because I have an errand to run (which means that my decision has been made and I thank you for your help, even if involuntary).

In this moment I am more pleased than ever to possess neither e-mail nor cell phone for I know that if I did, you would inundate me from all angles as soon as you read this letter . . .

Sending lots of hugs and kisses,

Your unreachable friend,

Maggy

P.S. This morning the Brittany sky was covered in clouds again, and this gray day that will unveil all the beauty of the landscape fills me with joy. Here, the blue sky always appears like an imposter that dazzles us with its violent and inappropriate contrasts that halo the South. Today, at least, I know all my thoughts will be calm, and that knowledge pleases me.

P.P.S. No man can understand the feminine sensibility, contrary to what we try to make ourselves believe sometimes. Your Julian is wide of the mark. That's fine. But his character on the whole is a true blessing. You know at any given moment where his mind is at, and he was always there when the floor gave way beneath your feet. And besides, what do we expect from men if not that endlessly verified certainty that they can never understand us?

RUE DES MORILLONS, JULY 11, 2016

You sly little fox!

I know the reason for your indecision, no thanks to you! What have you gotten yourself into? Can you explain to me what you are up to with Mr. Grant? And don't tell me that I am responsible for this relationship, because I will deny it flat out! When I think of that modern, feminist discourse about your desire for isolation and solitary strolls far from men and the constraints they impose on women! Aren't you ashamed?

You have to answer me as soon as possible to reveal what "that seductive man with the irresistible gaze" (those are your words!) is doing in Finistère. And don't lie to me, for I will see that rascal soon enough and I'll know how to make him talk. Will you at least tell me whether you left your hermitage for his gray eyes, for his delicious accent, or merely for his unbridled talent for adding lines to the ends of manuscripts found in the backs of attics?

Fine! I'll stop my accusations here and I'll wait for your version of the facts. But please, don't be too naïve, and remember that we're talking about a poker player whose principal strength is bluffing . . .

Despite everything I've just written you, I'm dying to meet this man who's coaxed my best friend out of her years-long exile.

Talk to you very soon, and don't be stingy with the details.

Your friend who's thinking of you,

Lisou

P.S. Remember that the inability to understand women affects British men too!

POINTE DES RENARDS, JULY 13, 2016

Hi Lisou!

Have you eaten your warnings? You know they were useless. I simply agreed, just to be nice, to serve as a guide for William during the three days he spent here, as he did for me when you parachuted me into London!

And anyway, I like to walk along the coastal paths at the first light of day and it turns out my guest also enjoys watching nature wake. We talked a great deal and I told him all about your latest obsession. Excited about this adventure, he asked me to guide him to Roscoff, where we found our bartender and his ladylove. On Sunday night all four of us ate together in a restaurant.

I thought of you; you would have loved this meeting between people from all over who never would have crossed paths without your matchmaking. So, despite your insistent and incorrect allusions to my relationship with our devastatingly charming Anglo-Franco-Belgian, thank you for these lovely encounters you've set in motion. William has changed his plans and sends his excuses. He won't stop in Paris after all. He went straight back to Lozère to conduct further research concerning your author before heading back to Belgium and then setting off for the United States, where he will participate in a poker tournament.

He is as enthusiastic as you are about the idea of solving this mystery, but when I spoke to him about those lines he added, he sealed up like an oyster . . . He told me he was a lover of poetry, but his tone was so fake that I thought he might be the worst liar I'd ever met! (Do you think I should try my hand at poker?)

There you have it, my dear Lisou, the full story you've been waiting for. It's true that I hesitated before opening the door of my hideout to a person I knew nothing about, or almost nothing. I finally decided to get over my suspicion, and I don't regret it. We spent three wonderful days together; my guest was always very considerate and kept a comfortable amount of distance. Also, I can't remember hosting a less invasive person than William. The first night, he cooked alongside me and we discussed children's literature. I told him about my profession and I introduced him to *Where's Waldo?* (we even searched for the little red gentleman for at least an hour!). William is probably the only Englishman not to know who Martin Handford is (perhaps his Belgian side is to blame) and I remedied that state of affairs. On the other hand, he is unbeatable when it comes to other Anglo-Saxon authors. Before he left, he wanted us to go eat on the coast with a thermos of coffee and a few crêpes. We were there for the sunrise, alone facing the landscape that transforms in each moment. We were sitting across from a somber and brooding sea. After our first cup of coffee, it was covered with golden wavelets, and by the time we left, it had donned that steel armor that suits it so well.

Thanks to you, I met someone unusual (I mean, we're talking about a poker player!) but very interesting, who I am sure I will keep in touch with in the months to come. So forget your unlikely ideas and instead look into whether you're available on the dates I've suggested below, for your beer-bottle-cap figurine increased my desire to visit Brussels tenfold . . .

More very soon,

Your still-solitary friend,

Maggy

P.S. Is it true that you bought Bastien a nearly two-foot-tall *Manneken Pis*? Did you give it to him in the middle of a meeting or did you casually place it on his desk during a coffee break?

from Anne-Lise to Sylvestre

RUE DES MORILLONS, JULY 14, 2016

Dear Sylvestre,

I would be thrilled to be your first reader and I am glad to know we are not on bad terms.

Because I have a few vacation days to take, I'm thinking of heading to Brussels with a friend. Since I can't be gone for too long, I will resist the tempting portrait you've painted of the beaches in the South and I will return to the office at the beginning of August. Then, three weeks later, I'll go supervise my son's move into his student apartment. So I'll spend the last days of the month painting (walls, don't get too excited) and building furniture sold in a kit by the Nordic people with their twisted sense of humor . . .

The quest that brought us together is on hold for now, even if Mr. Grant has promised to do a bit of investigating into his family. But your book has the power to connect people, there's no doubt about it, and you have to live with this responsibility. So I am curious to know the subject of your next novel: Can you give me a hint to tide me over until it's in my hands?

From where I'm writing to you (on the little desk in my office, in a slanting ray of inspiring morning sun), my view looks out onto a

Parisian garden with a very beautiful tree. For several weeks now, every time I look at it I've practiced the meditation exercise you taught me (that's what it is, right?) and which, I have to admit, brings me a comforting sense of well-being. Is that your secret? Your Folivora sensibilities are fed by exercising your full consciousness in order to grasp the world around you in complete serenity? And above all, were you thinking of this practice when you said this, thirty years ago:

> I was walking behind her and observing her, in complete quiet. I had no desire to flaunt her as my property nor to cry out to the world "this woman is mine," no. It was enough for me to look at her at any hour of the day, in the morning sun or the calming twilight, and to rediscover her at each moment through her unexpected movements which rendered her unfamiliar to me once again.

I hope you'll tell me the end of that brief romance one day. You left me unsatisfied by implying that the true story is less interesting than the one invented by our Waldo. But I'll stop asking you questions now, for I fear that my curiosity will cause you to grow distant once again, and nothing matters to me more than your mailman's well-being . . .

Your friend,

Anne-Lise

P.S. What lost world do you live in that the post office employees have no vehicle and can only access their routes via home invasion? No wonder people choose to communicate by e-mail!

P.P.S. The family drama is nearly forgotten. I don't speak about your novel at home anymore, even though I'm often thinking of it.

BELLE POELLE, GÉNOLHAC, JULY 14, 2016

Dear Anne-Lise,

Addressing you by name might seem a bit too familiar to you, but I cannot call you "madame" after hearing so many stories about your childhood from Maggy. I'm in my farmhouse in Lozère and if you could see me right now, you would see that I'm covered in spiderwebs, dirty as a rat and slovenly as could be, because I've spent the last three days back in the family house emptying each box and every drawer from the cellar to the attic. When I explain that my mother is a person who never throws away anything, and that she's kept this habit going for twenty years straight, you'll have an idea of the task I have set for myself.

The last time any tidying happened in this house was after my father's death, twelve years ago. I wanted to convince my mother to come live with me (at the time I had a more stable profession and I was living in the suburbs of London), but she never felt at home in England and preferred to live near her family in Belgium.

So we rented her an apartment in Brussels not far from where you stayed. I'll skip the details; just know that this is where our novel appeared. In fact it's while I was moving my father's things that I found the book. For a time I thought he might have been the author, but having never seen a typewriter in the house, I soon abandoned that idea.

Before I could ask my mother about the origin of this novel, her mental health deteriorated, definitively cutting her off from the surrounding world. During her moments of lucidity, she often expressed the desire to return to this house in Lozère where she had lived with my father. So I gave in to her desires and brought her here, making frequent trips to be sure she was doing well. Each time I exiled myself in this place (it is indeed tucked away, and Maggy can testify to this if she agrees to come visit me), I enjoyed picking up the book and scribbling a few lines in it before going to sleep.

So, for almost seven years now, my mother hasn't returned to our world. She lives in a specialized institution half an hour away from the farmhouse. I can't help her as much as I would like, but her old neighbors are nearby and visit her each week.

You must be wondering why I'm telling you all of my familial misfortunes when we don't even know each other. I'm getting to that. While tidying some papers, I found some photographs taken during a meal in 1996. My parents and several friends are celebrating an unknown event, and in one of the snapshots, your manuscript is visible on the garden table in the middle of all the glasses. I went to talk to my neighbors about it. To my great surprise, Bernadette (my mother's friend) burst into sobs upon seeing the photos. Her husband asked me to leave because she was not in a state to speak to me, which I had understood on my own; despite what they seem to think, I do possess a basic understanding of human emotions.

All that is to say, I would like for you to come to Lozère as soon as you can. I sense that you are silent because of your book, and my neighbors refuse to speak to me about any secrets concerning my family. Maggy praised your people skills and your way of getting all kinds of confessions out of people, and I sense that you would know better than me how to gain their trust. I promise you, the house is in very good condition and ready to welcome you. You can come with your entire family. We have plenty of rooms and three bathrooms. I have to be in the United States for ten days for work, but there is always a key at Bernadette's and you can make yourself at home here. I told Maggy all about it, and I'm certain she will find the same peace here as in her village. Nevertheless, I'm afraid she won't come, so I'm asking you, dear Anne-Lise, to convince her to come with you.

I am aware that this request is strange, and I am not the type of man who usually opens his door to people he barely knows, but after all, the way we met is at least as crazy as my proposition. For a while now I've given free rein to my feelings and my spontaneity long before considering what is reasonable, and today my instinct is telling me that this is the right thing to do.

I hope you will agree so we can finally meet, here in this house that was home to the object of your research for a number of years.

Faithfully yours,

William Grant

RUE DES MORILLONS, JULY 17, 2016

My dear Maggy,

Swap out the clothing in your luggage, because I took the liberty of changing our holiday plans. Brussels will have to wait, because our presence is requested in Lozère! We will substitute chocolate for chestnuts and beer for Quézac water.

I can hear your cries and shouts from here so I'll leave some blank space in my letter where you can be angry with me as much as you like . . .

Better? Now can I explain myself?

Yesterday morning I heard from your charming visitor. He might have a lead about who brought the manuscript to his parents' house. As you know, he is leaving soon for the United States, but he has entrusted us with the keys to his house so that we can continue the investigation on site. The place sounds magnificent and we'll bring along Katia, who is on summer break and doesn't know how to occupy her days (I suspect my beloved of using her as a chaperone, for, despite his claims, he is still worried about my involvement with this novel. So I happily accepted her presence, which will keep me above all suspicion).

So much so that I decided Sylvestre will accompany us. We will spend the first few days without William, but he will join us for the weekend. It's about time I saw for myself the power of his gray eyes over the female species. He was so insistent that I bring you with me that I get the sense your relationship is not as restrained as you would have me believe, and I am not convinced that we can offer the help he claims to justify our presence, when he seems completely capable of getting what he wants from people . . .

So, don't make me wait; tell me if you're coming to Paris so that we can travel together or let me know if you prefer to go to Lozère alone.

Answer quickly!

Kisses,

Lisou

P.S. Don't pout, I already know this trip will be incredible!

P.P.S. Note that I made no comment on your last letter nor on its main topic . . . On the contrary, I acted as if it were completely normal for my best friend to wax poetic about a sunrise she's already seen a thousand times and for her to use a teenager's vocabulary to share her morning observations . . . Do you think the sunrises will be as beautiful in Lozère?

from Anne-Lise to Sylvestre

RUE DES MORILLONS, JULY 18, 2016

Dear Sylvestre,

I left three messages on your answering machine! Is it not working? Did you program it to erase all messages from Paris? Or, more likely, do you simply refuse to come to Lozère alone or with your spouse?

Don't tell me you still haven't told her!

We leave on Wednesday, July 27, and I am repeating my offer to drive there together. In case the thought of three women chatting for seven hours on the road is too much to bear, I'll give you the address where we will be for a week. I'm bringing my daughter (she's been running in circles around the apartment since her brother left for vacation) and William Grant assured me that the house is very big. It's a farmhouse typical of the Cevennes region, built on the side of a hill. It's surrounded by hundred-year-old trees and in the autumn they produce the best chestnuts in Lozère!

Join us and we will finally have the pleasure of speaking without relying on the infallible speed of your mailman.

See you soon.

Best wishes,

Anne-Lise

P.S. In case it wasn't clear (or if you are one of those men who doesn't know how to read between the lines), let me be clear that I will be very upset if you do not respond to this letter . . .

RUE DES MORILLONS, JULY 19, 2016

Dear William,

Thank you for this invitation. It touches me more than I can say, even if, through Maggy, I already know how attached you are to this manuscript. The unbearable heat bearing down on the capital makes the idea of a trip to Lozère more appealing than ever.

So I will be there, along with my sixteen-year-old daughter, who is on summer break. I hope your gray eyes will charm her and encourage her to be on her best behavior. She is in a rebellious stage and makes fun of how I spend my free time and who I spend it with (don't repeat these words to Maggy or she will tear my eyes out, and I'm rather attached to them, believe it or not, even if they're only brown). To be honest, I hope that being around strangers will make her nicer and more open to the interests of those older than the age of sixteen . . .

As for our dear friend, I can assure you she will be there, even if she'll put up a bit of resistance at first to preserve her pride. As you now know, she has a tendency to run for her life as soon as a man takes a step in her direction. However, I suspect she has a weakness for multilingual globetrotting amateur poker players, who knows why! (Of course, all this remains between us and won't be of any interest to you unless you happen to have a penchant for hermits incapable of stringing two English words together.)

I have to warn you that I've also invited Sylvestre Fahmer. I haven't heard back from him yet, but I hope he will want to meet his readers, who were also the successive and illicit owners of his book.

You must find me shameless to bring all my family and friends to your house in Lozère, but I am very involved in this story and that entanglement alone justifies my loss of all decency. I hope to make a better impression when we finally get to meet.

As soon as the plans are set, I will send you the day and time of our arrival so that you will be able to alert your neighbors.

Thank you for organizing this trip.

Best wishes,

Anne-Lise

P.S. I am sending this letter to the address of the hotel you sent me, but because I have very limited confidence in the Americans and in trans-Atlantic mail delivery, I will confirm our arrival by phone.

from Maggy to Anne-Lise

Hi Lisou!

The blank space you left in your last letter was not nearly enough to contain my anger. What's gotten into you? What's with these vacations surrounded by strangers? We wanted quality time among friends and instead you've planned a Club Med parody! I will not play the role of ambassador and I won't think twice about abandoning you if the environment becomes intolerable. And so I will drive there in MY car, ready to flee at the first opportunity. And if William really wants me to be there, why didn't he write to me about it himself? I fear you are imposing this rendezvous on me the same way you're imposing it on your author and your daughter . . . What will our host think of such an invasion?

After thinking about it, I think I'd be better off contemplating the sun's reflection on the surface of the water from here, and cider appeals to me far more than Quézac water. If I do come, it will only be to protect your daughter, who, in a state of utter insanity, you've invited to a stranger's house along with Sylvestre, whom you've never met . . . You of all people should know that authors are generally unbalanced and unusual characters and that it's better to read their novels than spend time with them: it's not necessarily ideal, but it's certainly less involved and less risky!

And Julian? He's okay with you traveling to these far-flung regions, he doesn't protest? Unless you're using my presence as your cover . . . Lisou, I feel like I'm fifteen years old again, lying to your parents so you can meet Roland at a café! Remember how all that ended: your sneaky meeting turned out to be a bowling competition and you returned furious and humiliated because you lost!

As for William, you were not very clear about his words and I wish you wouldn't play matchmaker when you know very well there is no place for a man in my life. And when I think about it, perhaps I exaggerated the power of his gray eyes. I think that amidst the chestnuts, they will stand out less than on the seashore, and I advise you to keep all references to this subject to yourself.

If you have new information to give me before we leave, I will be at Agathe's Saturday night; I promised to help her organize a birthday meal (don't worry, I won't be the one cooking). So you can call the hotel to tell me what our mission will be over there and what path we are supposed to follow into the heart of the Cevennes woods.

See you Saturday!

Sending kisses, despite everything,

Maggy

P.S. A piece of advice: Swing by the bowling alley for a few practice games, you never know . . .

from Sylvestre to Anne-Lise

LES CHAYETS, JULY 21, 2016

Were you chosen by evil spirits to disrupt the perfectly tranquil life of a fifty-something in need of distraction? When I see an envelope in my box (its contents are visible from the house, because I never fixed it after a northern wind ripped off its door), I feel slightly worried wondering what I will find in your letters.

And now you expect me to go to Lozère! To the home of a man that I don't know, to spend time with people I know nothing about, when they've invaded my privacy by reading something I wrote more than thirty years ago!

I'm not coming.

I thought my silence in response to your repeated calls made it clear. Apparently that's not the case and perhaps it's time, Anne-Lise, that you finally know who you're speaking to.

I was born in the Pyrenees. Where stone won every battle. It dominates every house, every tree, every man. Those who live there have resigned themselves to submitting to it because it witnessed their birth and it will see their death. Stone is their eternity. When we leave such a place, we carry with us the immobility of the rock and the rustling of the forest. You think you can contain nature living out the days of your city-slicker life, but every night it reenters the fray. Into your dreams it slips: the wildness of the wind blowing down from the summits, the force of the water rolling its sludge down into the valley, and the stories of men and their demons who made generations of little mountain dwellers tremble.

My parents had two children. The first they named Pierre, the second, Sylvestre. Those two first names say it all. My brother was smart enough to stay. When we grow up in the shadow of mountains, we do not feel at home in metro stations. We try to get through it. Until one day, the body rebels. For me, that happened when I reached fifty years old. The first time I fainted was underground, between the Pyrénées and Belleville stations. First hospitalization. They alluded to burnout as a result of strenuous hours and long journeys in public transit. The second time I fainted, they advised me to get a car and opt for the relative quiet of traffic jams. The third time, the company therapist intervened so I'd be able to work remotely, in the cool of the early mornings near the gray stone. Because my wife works in Paris, we couldn't go back to the Pyrenees. So we withdrew to the north, at a reasonable distance from the capital. We bought an old house facing the horizon. In this hamlet where the land is affordable, a few scattered huts house depressed city-dwellers linked to the world by their high-speed Internet or destitute retirees living their last days as cheaply as possible.

Once I was nestled in the heart of nature, the dizzy spells became more infrequent, but I had definitively exhausted my human capital. I could no longer tolerate people. For a long time, I concealed this handicap from those close to me by claiming that chronic fatigue confined me to the village, then to the house. The horizon drew closer . . .

Stifled by that enclosure, my wife and my daughter fled, each on the arm of a savior. My affliction worked its way into my life in an insidious manner and it wasn't until it destroyed my family that I finally confronted it.

So I had to push my boundaries. Alone. For two years now, I've inched back toward civilization. I exchange two or three sentences with my neighbors and I can drive my car again, as long as I avoid big cities and human contact. I am what they call antisocial.

I would have liked to come to Lozère. Truly. I would have gone alone. During our years together, I never discussed that part of my life with my wife. This attitude will seem juvenile to you coming from a man of my age, but it's because I know that no woman (nor any man, I can assure you) wants to learn that she was chosen because her husband lost all hope of finding the love of his youth again one day.

Don't think I'm a bad person; I'm not saying that I regret the years spent or the joy experienced with my partner and my daughter; I will admit that the love I described and which so moved you has not manifested in my life since that time long ago when I wrote those pages. I am sure that my wife would have been perceptive enough to understand that if I had put this text in her hands. But there is no chance of that happening now, since we've been separated for four years . . .

I know that I wasn't clear about this, and I don't deny creating false allusions to a family life. Since your first letter, I thought that a correspondence with a single man would cause more problems for you than a literarily motivated discussion with a married man who is supposedly stable. Since I wanted to continue writing to you, I preferred to keep quiet about my situation. I was silent about my affliction and my isolation for the same reason.

I fulfill my professional obligations at my own pace and without any administrative oversight. The reports I submit aren't read for several weeks, and I assume from this that my work no longer holds much value for the firm that employs me. I suspect the human resources manager has found a dead-end street for a deranged individual. I'm not bitter. One day, I might even start to develop a limitless admiration for a society so organized that it has a solution for each problem, a lid for each pot, and an administrative pigeonhole for each individual, no matter the irregularities they develop . . .

There you have it. Now you will better understand my inability to join you in Lozère. I will be with you in spirit but I cannot do more than that.

Sylvestre

RUE DES MORILLONS, JULY 23, 2016

Dear Sylvestre,

Thank you for entrusting me with what you shared in your last letter. I found it very moving, and once more you've managed to make me smile . . .

Men always think they can triumph over their roots . . . that's not the case. Our roots infiltrate us from birth and we gain nothing by trying to hide them. Now that you've accepted it, can't you move forward, even if it means dragging around your past? Do you need to live in permanent confinement to hear the sound of the wind and feel the power of nature? And even if you do, come to Lozère! I called William, who confirmed what I suspected: the hamlet we'll be in is only four houses, one of which is occupied full time . . . His farmhouse is very large and extends down a slope as fine as the summits of the Pyrenees. On the inside of the house, there are lots of rooms and you can have an entire wing to yourself to escape to if our chatting becomes unbearable. This place was made for you, Sylvestre, so bring along your misanthropy and act like a curmudgeon, it won't be an issue. Once there, you'll find unusual people whose wounds are real even if you don't know about them yet. We can't move forward in life without getting some scars along the way. Come see us, and you'll feel less alone in your sadness.

If you come by car, you will drive through a silent country, full of scattered villages forgotten by the capital and you will see that there exists an entirely different France from the one of those people who spend their Sundays at Auchan or their paid leave on the beaches of the South. Seeing all of this might do you a world of good . . .

We are preparing your room. See you next week.

Your friend,

Anne-Lise

BLOSSOM AVENUE, FLUSHING, JULY 24, 2016

Dear Anne-Lise,

I'm thrilled that you're planning this trip to Lozère and I will make sure to get through all my meetings as quickly as possible. I am excited by the idea of a trip shared by book lovers . . . I told my neighbor, and she is happy to have people nearby for a few days and will figure out getting permission for my mother to leave. Each time she returns to her house I hope she will have a flash of memory that will return her to me for at least a few hours . . . So far, that's never been the case.

I take it that Maggy spoke to you about me, which makes me quite happy. If my gray eyes brought me moderate success at twenty years old, they are no longer enough to guarantee me the attention of women. I hope to be noticed more for my mind and my kindness than for the color of my gaze.

Over the last few days, I've realized that I do have a certain appreciation for those in exile incapable of pronouncing two words of English, and it's incredible that it's taken me so long to realize it . . . I know I can trust you to keep these words far from the ears of the one who might be frightened by them . . .

See you very soon,

William

P.S. As you can see, mail manages to fly over the Atlantic no matter the direction of the wind, and I remain convinced that it reaches me faster here than when I am hidden away in Lozère! I'm trying, by writing to you at Belle Poelle, to show you the charms of the Americans, who are not in reality how you think of them in France, with, let's say, that ancestral condescension toward all those countries lacking a few centuries of history . . .

BELLE POELLE, JULY 30, 2016

My Julian,

This trip is lovely!

I know you get daily updates from Katia, who uses and abuses her cell phone as soon as she thinks she's out of my sight, and believe me, you would have loved being on this vacation with us. For three days now, we've lived in this farmhouse in Lozère like a post-1968 commune (don't worry, minus the orgies and the drugs!). William is charming. He arrived two nights ago, two days earlier than we expected. He matches perfectly with the image I had in mind. He's a very handsome man, with a smooth face and groomed hands. He possesses a natural distinction that the French typically associate with English lords. He pampers everyone and I have to admit that his clear gaze can turn the heads of romantic souls (which is not me, don't worry).

And you won your bet: Sylvestre joined us yesterday morning. However, we were both wrong about his appearance. He is as somber as William is luminous. While we had imagined him as a pale and sickly man, used to working at night and hiding away during the day, there suddenly arrived a tall, strapping fellow with tanned skin shadowed by a three-day beard. Despite his outdoorsman physique, he doesn't exude the quiet strength we anticipated. Probably because of his disheveled brown hair or his tormented gaze through immense and bottomless black eyes. For the first few hours, he was withdrawn and examined us in silence. Then together we reread the end of the manuscript, and the afternoon was a succession of ramblings on the identity of the second author.

Then William showed us the series of photographs from 1996. In one of them, you can in fact glimpse Sylvestre's book. It's open on the table as if someone had left it there to go get themselves an aperitif. To find out as much as I could, I gathered a small bouquet of flowers and went to invite the neighbors to dinner. That very night, there were eight of us at the table: their daughter Alice, who works in Alès as a librarian, came with them. I hit it off with her immediately and took advantage of a moment alone to tell her everything.

She read the novel that very night and brought it back to me this morning at breakfast. We had coffee together, the two of us wrapped up in our jackets, because, at this altitude, the mornings are cold. With a view of the waking nature and a magnificent lifting of the fog, Alice told me about the conversation she had with her mother last night.

The day the photo was taken, it was one of her uncles who had brought the book over. It was almost with relief that her mother finally told her about her younger brother, referred to as "poor David" by the entire family. Until then, merely saying his name was enough to put a stop to any conversation, clearly provoking Bernadette's sadness. Bringing up her baby brother had become taboo and so the younger generation hesitated to mention their uncle, who had clearly taken a wrong turn.

David was the youngest of seven boys and girls, and Bernadette, Alice's mother, was the eldest. When he was little, he was a gifted child. He had an ease with people and was brilliant in school. When he was eleven, the village teacher convinced his parents to send him to a boarding school in Alès, where he excelled in math and in literature. He was the only child of the family to get his baccalureate and everyone already imagined him as a lawyer. That excellence led him to Marseille to continue his law studies. In order to save money, he lived with a friend whom he'd met on the port where he unloaded boats for a bit of money. From then on, it seemed that the young, promising man found it more lucrative to associate with his roommate and his friends, who specialized in robbing villas. He was arrested several times, but his knowledge of the law allowed him to escape from overly harsh punishments for a while and his first prison sentences never exceeded a year. Until the day when the police went to arrest him at Belle Poelle, where he was charged with organizing a bank robbery . . .

Bernadette was even more traumatized than her brothers and sisters, because David had always been her favorite. Think of what she must have gone through when he received ten years in prison . . . Well, he didn't learn his lesson, because he went right back to his illegal activities when he got out, after eight years behind bars. Arrested again a year ago (now here's a man who follows through on his ideas; nothing can deter him from his choice of career!), he is currently detained at the Villeneuve-lès-Maguelone, where he has several more months to go.

Talk about unusual characters: first a poker player, now we have a bank robber!

In any event, there hasn't been a family reunion since the dramatic arrest of the baby brother. Bernadette remembers the day when David gave the manuscript to William's mother; sharing a passion for literature, the two of them talked about the book as they made dinner. After that, of course, Bernadette forgot all about it and never asked David about the book, which means we don't know how the novel arrived in his possession . . .

Yesterday, William's mother spent the day with us. She was pleasant company, despite her distant gaze, which, though it's the same color as her son's, has lost all its vivacity. She sat for a while near the window that looks out onto Mount Lozère, a half smile on her lips, erased at regular intervals by an expression of inexplicable panic. She doesn't speak; words stay blocked behind her lips, which she keeps tightly shut as if she feared the words might escape her. The only time we saw her liven up was when Sylvestre took out his manuscript and placed it on the table. Then something incredible happened: the old woman got up from her armchair to take it. She stared hard at it for several minutes, then she started to caress the cover while chanting the name "David." All discussion stopped in the large room; we were stunned by this newfound energy. How can a recollection still slither through the haze of a mind without memory?

William gently took the pages from the hands of his mother, who smiled a final time before sinking back into her own world. In that moment, the story of the manuscript seemed far away; we were all lost, panicked, like her perhaps, at the idea of this illness lying low in the shadows, ready to swallow us up, too, at the bend of the road. The disease that eats away memory is surely the most awful of all, because it erases our past day by day, making us disappear little by little, until we've never existed.

Despite the difficulties we encountered, you can see the progress we've made, since we managed to figure out the book's journey up to 1996 after Sylvestre lost it in 1983. You see, our unfailing determination has paid off and we are able to brazenly turn back time. Don't worry, I don't plan to visit the Villeneuve-lès-Maguelone prison; I've delegated that task to William, who's promised to see about visiting as soon as he's back in Brussels (he leaves Tuesday night; he's quite the traveler).

You realize this book's journey is so extraordinary there could be a novel written about it?

As our beloved daughter must have told you, we're leaving Tuesday morning to avoid the weekend traffic (she's been so sweet to me since we arrived in this house, I think she appreciates the ambiance of the place, and if only for the pleasure of seeing her smile again like when she was a child, I absolutely do not regret this trip to Lozère).

Can you prepare a nice big meal for us that night? We've been eating very well since our arrival here (yes, yes, even Katia).

XO,

Your Lisou

from William to Anne-Lise

Dear Anne-Lise,

I learned something earth-shattering yesterday that I absolutely must share with you.

After you left for Paris, I left Belle Poelle and went to Belgium to speak with my cousin, Ilana. She had been close with my mother, and I was hoping that their relationship would allow her to explain my mother's astonishing reaction to the manuscript. My cousin knew something; it was clear from the way she lowered her head and blushed. I had to beg for nearly an hour before she finally agreed to talk to me about it!

Ilana is my age. As children, we spent our vacations together at my maternal grandmother's house. We grew up far from each other, but each summer was the opportunity for joyous reunions and I kept no secrets from her. I'm not sure whether the inverse was true, because Ilana is one of those people who always listens to others and never speaks about herself. She could have been a nun, but she became a psychologist who treats children and teens. She lives only for her job; she was never married and didn't want to have a family. Make no mistake, she's the most joyful person I know and she's always surrounded by friends and loved ones. Helping them is her greatest joy.

Naturally, she supported my mother after my father passed away. They lived on the same street, and saw each other every day, and her presence reassured me. Before getting sick, my mother opened up to Ilana and told her all about her life. I never asked her to tell me her memories—I probably thought I had time . . .

I confess that what Ilana told me disturbed me. David gave this manuscript to my mother, but it was not a simple book exchange. He was in love and the feeling was mutual . . . He was forty-six, my mother fifty-five when David's imprisonment separated them. According to my cousin, their romance began a year and a half earlier, during a meal at Bernadette's. Ilana spoke of love at first sight and assured me that the two wrote to each other for a long time before giving in. Also, according to her, if my mother wanted to return to Lozère before getting sick, it was partially because the letters from her beloved were saved in a chest there.

I never saw the chest in the farmhouse, but I'm going there next week to have another look. I hate what I'm about to do, believe me when I say that, Anne-Lise, but I need to know the truth, and the scene we witnessed seems to corroborate my cousin's story.

I didn't tell Maggy my plan because I imagine she'll be outraged at my indiscretion. In Belle Poelle, I forced myself to keep my distance. And that took a lot of energy because I couldn't get a read on her charming but detached demeanor . . . If you have any insight into her feelings, please enlighten me . . .

On my end, I will keep you up to date about my discoveries (because after all, this "chest" could in fact be one of the old wooden trunks stashed in the attic!).

I know that I'm distancing myself from your literary quest. I hope that you will not be angry with me for having chosen you as a confidante now that certain parts of my past are crumbling like the neglected vestiges of an abandoned family house.

Your friend,

William

P.S. You can write me back in Lozère, because I don't think I will stay here more than three days . . . Too many questions lure me back to France once more.

P.P.S. Your cousin? Still alive?

from Anne-Lise to Maggy

My dear Maggy,

Did you arrive back home safely? And how are you tolerating your isolation after such a delicious adventure in communal life?

On Thursday morning I had a hard time getting back into all the projects I had ditched on my desk that I have to submit to my cousin before the 13th. For the first time in two years, I passed him in the hallway without feeling the urge to gouge his eyes out. However, he hasn't changed. He walks around like a young dynamic executive (past his prime with his gray temples), his two cell phones in hand, constantly holding his MacBook Air, which always seems to supply an adequate response to any question asked. He measures his success by the number of tweets about him and only gets his news on social media . . . No doubt you would love him; I'll introduce you whenever you want.

Fortunately, the transformation of my daughter made up for that unpleasantness. Even you observed just how good the trip to Lozère was for her; in fact, the metamorphosis continues in Paris. She has been a different Katia since returning home. She's always smiling, and although she still considers housework an awful activity, she now shows an interest in my hobbies and in the people I spend time with. She won't stop talking about Sylvestre and William, as if they were members of the family. The latter, especially, made a strong impression on her; she absolutely wants us to return this winter to see Lozère covered in snow . . . I agree with you, that man's gaze possesses something magical that has transformed my rebellious daughter into a civilized adolescent.

I will be sure to thank him when I answer the letter I've just received. I will remain discreet about its contents, but the astonishing discoveries that he's made render the saga of this novel more and more extraordinary.

Be aware that all these events have worn him down and, if you write to him, hit pause on your constant irony . . .

More very soon, my dear Maggy.

Enjoy the sea air,

Kisses from your Lisou

P.S. I just received a message from Bastien about a project we're working on together. It's 11:50 P.M. on a Saturday! Does that man never sleep? He must get that hyperactivity from his mother's genes, because on our side, the whole family requires eight hours of sleep and two liters of coffee before taking on the smallest task . . .

POINTE DES RENARDS, AUGUST 10, 2016

My dear Lisou,

You were right, our little adventure did me a world of good and I've practically finished the second volume of the adventures of Croco: *Croco Leaves His Island*. I only have two more illustrations to go. I already know you'll laugh reading page 23 . . . there's an allusion to the mission we set out on when we were ten years old. Remember that we suspected your neighbors of hiding a body underneath their terrace pavers and we would watch them through a pair of binoculars (which didn't magnify anything in the slightest . . . I think they were a prize your parents won at a gas station)!

That said, your last letter left me hanging. What is this new mystery you mention but won't say anything about? Despite your insinuations, I haven't heard from William since my return to Finistère. Our poker player only took the time to write to you, and so you know about him more than me . . .

I can only assume the attraction you imagined between us is unfounded, and that's a relief. I am now free from distracting thoughts. That man is a will-o'-the-wisp and I don't want to end up like those voyagers carried away by lost souls, right in the heart of Brittany . . . Do you at least know where he is at the moment? With all his moving around, I don't know whether he's gone back to Lozère or if he's returned to the English capital, and I left the notes for my next project at his farmhouse. If he contacts you, can you please tell him that I would very much appreciate him sending them back to me?

I am very happy to learn that your daughter's wonderful attitude has continued. I found her lovely during our trip, and I'm sure you exaggerate her phobia of household chores. I remember she helped prepare all the meals we shared there. On several occasions, I caught her in a heated discussion with Sylvestre, whose reserved nature she vanquished before any of us. Without Katia's presence, our dear author would have taken much longer to tell us his story.

He's a man who deserves to be known but I am not one to criticize his preference for solitude. And his sincerity touched me when he spoke of his difficulties, even if it was only implied.

Since you're starting to think of winter vacation, might you have some time for us to finally take that trip to Brussels? I don't want to steal you away from your family, but it would be nice for the two of us to finally take the getaway we've been dreaming of for three years without our schedules ever matching up . . . With both of our birthdays in October, it could be a magnificent opportunity to celebrate together.

I'm signing off now so I can finish my illustrations. Give a big kiss to the children and to Julian . . .

Your friend who doesn't send a hug because she's covered in paint,

Maggy

P.S. Now the wind is picking up and making the rain crash against my windows. Will you think I'm strange if I tell you that this weather makes me smile for no reason?

P.P.S. I applaud the great wisdom that has guided you to go easy on your cousin. But I still miss the times when you were more belligerent and the happiness I felt reading about all the suffering you dreamed of inflicting on him. If you change your mind, I've set aside a few methods of torture I discovered in a noir novel that describes the deliriums of a serial killer with great pleasure.

RUE DES MORILLONS, AUGUST 11, 2016

Dear Sylvestre,

For the last week I have been drowning again in the demands of the office and I've realized that I love going to work in August. That novelty, August workers in the capital, is a real pleasure. Have you experienced this feeling? It's as though we're outside of time and we stroll in our suits and nice clothes through the Parisian streets, a grin of superiority on our faces when we pass the tourists in their shorts. We display our condescension like castle owners who tolerate photographs of their fiefdom before escorting them to the exit. Although we remain available to help direct lost vacationers, we keep, behind our smiles, the alert eye of people in a hurry who are permanently squinting at their cell phones. And that attitude gives us the importance we lack the rest of the year. Excuse this little quirk that I confess with shame and let me deliver the latest updates.

We can no longer ask William to visit David. Family events have now overlapped with the journey of our book and I think our friend needs to take a step back from our search. So I will go myself, and I beg you to come with me to the Villeneuve-lès-Maguelone prison.

I know you will shake your head reading these words, but I

also sense, despite everything, your indulgent smile . . . Oh yes, I observed you during those few days in Lozère and I believe you are no longer the same since you opened my original package. You spent those few days with us without visibly suffering from our presence. You spoke of your illness when you didn't have to. And you confided in me, on the last day, about the happiness you felt from our conversations.

A man who has rediscovered the taste for life because he has rediscovered his manuscript . . . Nothing is trivial, Sylvestre, as you know, and I sense you are prepared today to move heaven and earth to discover your book's journey over the last thirty years. So I hope to have your support as I enter the doors of the Villeneuve-lès-Maguelone penitentiary. You are up to the task of this new challenge, I am sure of it.

I just have to tell Julian that I am leaving. I'm waiting to receive the response to my visit request before I face his incomprehension yet again. Two days ago, he asked me for the hundredth time why I refused to give up my share of the business (which is very small, don't get too excited) to my cousin. He even brought up what we could offer Katia and Matthias with the money from the sale! Sometimes I am surprised to find that this man, with whom I've shared my life for twenty-six years, is still astonished by my decisions and my stubbornness. Are couples always so poorly matched? Is it possible for each person in a pair to still possess, after more than two decades, a total ignorance of the other?

As for you, dear Sylvestre, don't leave me hanging; get ready for our trip to the South in order to spare your friend from facing the agonies of her first visit to prison alone.

Thanking you in advance for your support in this ordeal,

Your cellmate,

Anne-Lise

from Anne-Lise to William

Dear William,

I received a letter from Maggy this morning. I sense some bitterness and I think you should write to her as quickly as possible. Why haven't you already? She is annoyed that she didn't hear from you before I did and I don't want our friendship to suffer from misplaced jealousy. And please, dear William, don't ever reveal our private conversations about her, because when I look around, I see I don't have enough friends to be able to sacrifice one . . . Not even for the best of motives.

As for you, I can only imagine what a son must feel upon discovering his mother's romantic affair when there had never been any reason to suspect such a thing. The news must be all the more difficult to learn since it has arrived too late for you to be able to get any kind of explanation from her. But it's a private matter and we should forgive those close to us for missteps similar to those we have experienced or that we are still experiencing . . . And, most importantly, my dear William, don't lose sight of the fact that what awakens a sleeping heart is worth the effort. I know you understand what I'm saying . . .

Of course, I don't feel authorized to discuss this with Maggy or Sylvestre as I usually do. And so I leave you the task of informing them (or not) of these discoveries concerning your parents.

I impatiently wait to hear from you.

Your friend,

Anne-Lise

P.S. My cousin Bastien is still alive as of today—surprising, isn't it? But I have compiled a list of discreet elimination tactics in a red folder that I labeled "Save"! So keep an eye on the news! Our next disagreement could indeed be spread on the front page of the Parisian papers . . .

BELLE POELLE, AUGUST 16, 2016

Dear Anne-Lise,

I found it! After running from the basement to the attic and emptying everything that resembled a chest, I had abandoned all hope and was wandering from one room to another interrogating each object with my gaze as if it might have the power to reveal my mother's hidden life. Until I noticed her sewing basket, placed near the old leather armchair. It was originally my grandmother's, and you might have noticed it during your stay here. It's made of dark wood and opens to reveal treasures of multicolored threads, sequins of all sizes, and thimbles that have gone through the years without being any worse for wear.

When I was a child, I called it the treasure chest, and I would spend entire hours sorting the buttons while my grandmother knit near the fire.

This morning, it was so obvious; I unfolded the three levels of the box and I saw the corner of an envelope peeking out from under the tape measures. I pulled it out. It was actually a bundle. There were thirteen letters. All from him.

Would you believe me if I told you that I cried reading them? Probably. This is what David wrote in his last letter:

My love,

I told my friends that I would stop everything. I declared that I was officially abandoning this life and that nothing could make me change my mind, even if I had to clean floors or build walls out of cinder blocks eight hours a day to make us enough money to live. Nothing is more important to me—knowing that we will grow old together. Since you told me yes, I can't sleep anymore, I can't eat anymore, I can't live anymore . . . I simply wait for you.

I fixed up our escape den in the location you know and I moved my things there as well as the money we will live off of for a short time. These are my own savings; every dollar was earned honestly. Don't worry about anything, I bought that house and I know we will be happy there. You can come here as soon as you've spoken to your son. Tomorrow I'll slip the key into your mailbox, and all the property deeds are in your name. I want for you to feel at home. We will see each other Sunday during the family meal and I will give you that incredible book that describes so well what I feel for you . . .

See you very soon,

David

These words were written five days before his arrest. I will never know how my mother responded, but it is clear that she was going to leave with him and that everything was organized for their escape. They don't mention my father. Did he know something or would he have found out after the fact? And what about that house that David bought for them to escape to? Do you think he sold the property when he got out of prison? Did my mother go there alone to mourn her lost love? Finally, the book he mentions has to be Sylvestre's, don't you think? Since last night, all these questions have hammered at my mind like voodoo incantations.

But don't worry, I'm a big boy and after a brief, legitimate shock, I am now taking a much-needed step back. If I suffer, it's above all for my mother, when I imagine the hardship she must have experienced when David was arrested. Imagine, I suspected nothing of her despair when her beloved was incarcerated for several years . . . now I understand the changes that happened at that time. I had sensed a sadness that invaded my parents' home and I, caught up in my own worries, hadn't given it much thought.

You will see that I am an egotistical being, Anne-Lise, far from the voyager with the dreamy gaze that hosted you in Lozère. The past is catching up to me and reveals to you a man his loved ones could never count on, a person ready to flee when his family is in turmoil. Believe me, I regret it. That's why I haven't written to Maggy. I am not proud of the memories I hide behind this high-roller bon vivant persona, and I would never dare to impose them on a woman who, I sense, is in search of serenity and authenticity.

So I will go back to London, where I will stay for several months awaiting winter and the obligations that will then take me to Japan. I know how much you liked that region of Lozère; the keys are with my neighbors and you are free to hide away there whenever you like. Consider that house yours . . .

I've spoken only of myself, but I haven't forgotten Sylvestre. His manuscript is currently mixed up with my family history and that discourages me from accompanying you to meet David. Nevertheless, let me know if you find Waldo.

I have to tell you the truth now: despite your secrecy, Anne-Lise, I know what you do, I know the truth . . . I did a bit of research when I came back from Maggy's and what I discovered has allowed me to understand your stubborn persistence to help Sylvestre.

Hoping you reach the end of the road,

Your friend,

William

RUE DES MORILLONS, AUGUST 18, 2016

Dear William,

You've just discovered a secret part of your mother's life and I can tell you're unsettled by it. But at the time, you had your own boat to steer and even the most attentive son wouldn't have been able to imagine such an affair. By the way, if you had, what would you have done? Rushed to the aid of your mother who had lost her great love? Supported your father who had just learned that his wife was going to flee with a reformed thief? Would you have preferred to tear yourself between the two and add your suffering to their own?

No. You acted in the way that was best for your parents, who had no need for you to be involved in that private affair. At least, that's my humble opinion on the matter, and I am amazed to see you accuse yourself of wrongdoing, describing a William Grant who is cowardly and wishy-washy.

So this morning, reading you blame yourself this way, I had the strange feeling that you were toying with my ability to solve mysteries. I reread your letter, between the lines as they say, and I feel that your self-critique is alluding to parts of your existence that

I still don't know about. Unless you're referring to this life change that you mentioned in passing in Lozère?

You told us you were a literature professor in England before abandoning "everything" "from one day to the next" to become an international poker player . . . At my age, I understand that the expression "from one day to the next" leaves unsaid what happened between the two days, and it's clear that the night that separates these days was heavy with reflections and uncertainty!

You notice that we have the decency to not ask about "everything" that you have gotten rid of . . .

So, my dear William, be generous enough to finish the story and tell me what a friend needs to know in order to judge you appropriately! And you can count on me to do so with conviction if you truly deserve it.

As of today, I'm refusing to say that you are awful because of past mistakes that I know nothing about! So I'll wait for your indictment and, if you blame yourself, do it with eloquence and supporting evidence . . .

Awaiting your misdeeds,

Your friend (until further notice),

Anne-Lise

P.S. I don't know where you are and I'm trying my luck by sending this to you in London, but if you go back to Lozère anytime soon, you will notice that Maggy left behind a drawing for her next book that she would like to have sent back to her. Don't read into this too much, she really is that absentminded: I too have found some of her drawings in my bathroom and, when I go to her house, we spend a considerable amount of time each day chasing down her keys or her bag, as you must have experienced during your stay in Finistère . . .

P.P.S. You know who I am and I am delighted. I don't hide this information, it's just that I keep quiet about it—and I know that you will appreciate the difference.

from Sylvestre to Anne-Lise

LES CHAYETS, AUGUST 18, 2016

If my calculations are correct, you will receive this note on Saturday. I can see you already, reading my letter, lost in the contemplation of the park opposite your apartment, a cup of coffee in your hand, savoring the surrounding calm with each sip. I know you Parisians don't understand the meaning of the word "silence," but I was touched by your determination in Lozère to get up at dawn and take advantage of the early morning quiet.

Are you serious? You're inviting me to prison? As casually as when you dragged me through the Cévennes forests . . . At risk of surprising you, I will not say no. I am ready to come with you to meet this David who specializes in bank heists (admit that I have astonished you).

But I have to warn you that I will be away for the next few days. I'm leaving tomorrow to see my daughter. It is impossible for me to reschedule this, because this is part of her annual vacation. Yes, you read that correctly: I will brave the airport crowds, the agony of the flying coffin, and the terror that foreign faces inspire in me. I am taking the big leap. I am focusing on Coralie's joy when she learned that her father would finally visit her in her adopted home.

She is aware of the effort I am making and I will not disappoint her. For the second time, I will cross the ocean with my manuscript beneath my arms, but this time, it will be to have my daughter read it (and I will keep it within hand's reach for the entire trip, no risk of abandoning it beneath a seat even though it's now saved on three different USB drives) . . .

If I survive the grizzly bears and the maple syrup, I will be at your service starting August 27 to meet any unusual people you have come across and that you would like to introduce me to: a former wild cat tamer now trained in slug dressage, a former minister exiled at the bottom of an Irish grotto, a veterinarian specializing in the study of crickets, or a harmonica player from the Berlin philharmonic . . . I smile to myself thinking of all the incredible people who might have flipped through these pages before our thief and I wonder whether we will find one day the person you call Waldo.

Did I tell you that I am starting to become friends with my mailman? On Monday he came up to my door and he looked so happy to bring me my mail that I offered him a coffee. It was awkward at first, then our conversation became more fluid until we launched into an animated discussion on the turbulent relations between Poulet-Malassis and Baudelaire. When my guest noticed that an hour had passed and he would be late for the rest of his route, he took off, but we agreed to meet the next day to finish our friendly argument.

So here I am with a friend who's a mailman and a Baudelaire specialist who merits inclusion onto the list of all the exceptional people I've met thanks to you. These newcomers have settled so powerfully into my life that I have promised myself to tell my daughter about this wild journey. As soon as I set foot on Canadian soil, she will know all the details and I will not forget your part in this affair.

I'm waiting to hear your plan to organize our expedition to the South as soon as I return. I've already looked into it and we'll have to take the train to Montpellier and from there a bus will bring us to the prison in forty-five minutes. Remember, only a year ago, it took me hours to prepare for the tiniest trip to the village bakery! And now, prison . . . What an incredible adventure for a man who's never had to pay a single parking ticket!

Sylvestre

P.S. Did you see that we cannot wear watches, belts, and jewelry so as not to set off the metal detector? And that we have to reserve a visiting room, just like reserving a table at a restaurant?

AVENUE DU MOULIN-DE-LA-JASSE,

VILLENEUVE-LÈS-MAGUELONE, AUGUST 20, 2016

Madame,

I'm writing to let you know that I have refused the visit request you submitted. I don't know what you want from me, but at my age, I have a right to peace, no matter the reason I was sentenced.

If you are looking for the confession of a convict who can amuse the Parisian bourgeois by recounting his life behind bars, I know prisoners who would be delighted to flaunt their experience. Believe me, mine is not special and would not make for more than two lines in a tabloid. Bank robbery is not a heroic activity and the crooks who turn to it are not daring. If you want to hook your readers, you should invent a story about the thrills of a life of disgrace and the improbable myth of the reformed hero. In any event, I advise you to turn to other testimonials and I remain at your service to provide you with the names of prisoners who dream of starring in reality TV shows. If you avoid my colleagues who work in packaging sweets, there are some who are very presentable and who have kept a certain allure thanks to their diligent visits to the gym.

Thanking you in advance for your understanding upon reading this letter.

Sincerely,

Inmate 822

David Aguilhon

from William to Anne-Lise

My dearest Anne-Lise,

I had just opened the door to my London refuge when I saw your words awaited me. Here, I live in the English language, which is also the language of my past and the drama linked to it. So it is easier for me to tell you everything today.

As you already know, ten years ago, I was an English professor at Brunel University, to the west of London. What you don't know is that at the time, I was married and a father to an adorable little seven-year-old girl. I was happy without really being aware of it, which is often the case when we think our life is on track and that we will continue on in that way until the end of time.

Like many men who are over forty, I dreamed of changing my life, of tackling new challenges. When a young colleague started a poker club, I signed up and discovered the excitement of the game. I, who had never touched cards, quickly became a star on campus and, crowned with that reputation, I plunged into a romantic relationship with the person who had introduced this passion into my life. All of that is unfortunately dull, you will agree, dear Anne-Lise. But, caught up in the joy of rediscovered youth, I didn't think of the harm I would cause my family when she learned the truth.

The next part is even more common. My wife Moïra left me; she took off with our daughter to her parents' house in Scotland. Quick to counterattack, I quit my job and started to make the rounds of poker tournaments to earn my living. At the time, I thought our separation was temporary and I took advantage of my bachelor life with a certain pleasure. I went to tournament after tournament and I would go back to see my family haloed with the glory offered by money so easily won. I brought them elaborate gifts, but although Laura was still delighted by my visits, her mother resented me and our reunions were filled with hostility and anger.

July 12, 2008, two years after our separation, I received a message from my stepfather telling me that Moïra had been hospitalized after a car accident. I went to Scotland and found out that she was in a coma. She never came out of it. She died August 15.

My in-laws revealed to me that in the year that had preceded the car accident, Moïra had made two suicide attempts . . . they didn't need to spell it out for me to understand. Even if, for a time, I was mad at her parents for not having informed me of the gravity of the situation, I knew, deep down, that my wife never recovered from the breaking up of our family.

So I left the game and settled down in Scotland to devote myself to my nine-year-old daughter who had just lost her mother. We searched for a new equilibrium for the two of us and we lived together for three years. Occasionally I taught seminars but I had enough money to live without going back to my job as a professor. During that time, I took refuge in the manuscript. It had the curious power to diminish my pain and guilt. Until my mother-in-law suffered a heart attack and spent some time in the hospital . . . Convinced she had had a brush with death, she entrusted Moïra's last letter to her granddaughter. Reading it, Laura discovered that I was the cause of the depression that had destroyed her mother. At twelve years old, she packed her bags and left to live with her grandparents. Since that day, she has refused to see me or to speak to me on the phone.

I am not trying to make you feel sorry for me, Anne-Lise. I am not miserable and I provide my family with every possible material comfort. I know they are doing well and I get regular updates from my father-in-law, who remains the sole link between my daughter and me. I travel a lot, I meet incredible people like you and your friends, or like the members of the Belgian writing group, and I don't ask the forgiveness of anyone. If I am guilty of the death of my beloved wife, I am punished each morning waking up alone, without being able to experience the priceless joy of seeing my daughter grow up. That's why I was delighted to meet Katia, who is exactly the same age and who I watched with pleasure, thinking that Laura might resemble her.

There you have it; you know everything about my silences and the shadows that weigh on my life. Know that I'm still your friend.

Yours,

William

from Anne-Lise to David

Monsieur Aguilhon,

I thank you for personally telling me about your rejection of my visit request. However, I am neither a journalist, nor a writer, nor a producer of a TV series. My interest in meeting you is completely unrelated. The connection between our two existences is a book, written more than thirty years ago, and which you gave to Madame Grant, your sister's neighbor in Lozère.

The author of this text was reunited with it not long ago and seeks, with my help, to retrace its steps since it disappeared in 1983. Without knowing you, I believe you will grant our request the importance it deserves and I hope you will agree to tell us the name of the person who gave it to you.

You are the last known link in the chain of successive owners of this manuscript, which seems to have caused a veritable disruption in the lives of its readers. I completely understand your suspicion of me, but please know that the only motive for my request was to ask you about this.

I thank you in advance for any information you are willing to share about this novel.

Cordially,

Anne-Lise Briard

P.S. I want to assure you that there was no morbid curiosity on my part when I requested to visit you in prison. I was even briefly relieved to know that you refused my request, that's how nervous I am to enter a prison. My only motivation was to meet a person who had loved this book and who, because of that, already felt familiar to me.

from Maggy to William

Dear William,

I realize that I'm writing to you for the first time. It's been three weeks since we left Lozère and I have no idea how you've been doing. Well, that's only partially true, because your exchanges with Anne-Lise prove that you're at least still alive.

However, she didn't tell me a word of the revelations you made to her. Normally displaying the opposite of my secretive and silent behavior, she now shuts up like an oyster if I ask her anything about you. I don't dare imagine what you confided in her to provoke such a transformation. When I called her a few days ago (I have to be pretty worried to go all the way to the hotel and use that device which I so detest!), she responded with these words: "Write to him, please . . ."

You will agree that it's risky to contact a person whose struggles we do not know, and I immediately rejected her suggestion. Then, this morning, I went for a walk along the coastal roads. They no longer resemble highways, because the first drizzle chased the August vacationers inland, in the pursuit of Breton authenticity or waterproof ecomuseums. We still have a few local reserves subsidized by Tipiak. Between two menhirs, we can see old Breton women parade by in their traditional headdresses.

I thought again of those strolls we took when you came to Finistère. The morning breeze changed my mood and I realized that even without knowing what was bothering you, I could at least distract you by telling you the latest local gossip.

To start off, the small empty spot in the marketplace has a new buyer. Remember how we guessed at the various businesses that might go there? You had suggested a flute store that would attract players from all over the world, and I thought up a paint store that would sell only the color blue. Oil, watercolor, or pastel doesn't matter, but on the condition that we buy only the color of the sky, which here is often diluted with gray, as you remarked. We finally agreed on a stand that would display original manuscripts, on the condition that they had never been edited.

We were both wrong, because yesterday I discovered a poster that announced: "Souvenir shop, coming soon." And so the pipes, the tubes of paint, and the faded pages will give up their place to hangers adorned with shells, clocks decorated with Breton lighthouses, bowls from Quimper with the words "world's best dad," or charts that will teach you the recipe for *Kig ha farz* or explain the workings of marine knots. Of course, everything will be imported from China or Turkey, fabricated by small hands with no clue what region of the world Finistère is in. At least tourists will find a new meeting point directly on the way back from the shuttles that connect Ushant to the continent.

I don't feel any bitterness or miss the village as it was in my childhood. I observe these evolutions with suspicion, of course, but also with a certain pleasure—at the idea that nothing is unchangeable, that the Earth will continue to turn in our absence despite the numerous predictions about the end of the world in our lifetime.

Did you know that I finished my illustrations? I am very happy with them; I think they're better than the illustrations in the first volume and it's a real relief to find that we can age and improve. After being told *aging is a shipwreck*, we would be tempted to believe that all our faculties deteriorate with time. This is not true, and I have the proof on my desk. The second installment of the adventures of Croco is more elaborate than the first. (As promised, I will send you a copy as soon as it's out.)

On that note, perhaps you found the folder that I left in Lozère, which contains a preliminary draft of my next book? If so, you can keep it, because I decided to change the animal protagonist. I chose the name of my new character from a novel I just read: he will be named Muffin and he will be a very peculiar puffin. I love this stage, where I come up with the main storyline and where I am allowed to be bold. There is a freedom in this work that enchants me.

I can see black clouds approaching from the west in the distance and it makes me smile. This stormy weather on its way is synonymous with working inside, a mug of tea in my hand, cradled by the sound of the wind because the few remaining walkers will take refuge in the village crêperies. On that note, sniff this letter before putting it away: I'm sure you'll smell the lovely odor of crêpes that perfumes my entire house, because I made about twenty just now. That will be my lunch, my snack (I remember that seeing me have my snack like a child greatly amused you), and perhaps even my dinner . . .

There you have it, dear William, anecdotes aimed at distracting you for a bit from the worries that seem to control you. When you are isolated like I am here, nature overrides the human concerns that then become futile and pathetic. If one day you feel lost in the bustling life of the big cities of this world, take a break and come see me at the tip of Brittany; you will see the horizon remains constant, no matter our suffering.

Here's hoping that I made you smile a bit, sending a hug.

Your friend,

Maggy

from David to Anne-Lise

Madame Briard,

Please accept my apologies. I just read your letter and I admit I find it very hard to trust people since I've been shut up in here. It's true that in the last fourteen years I've received requests for interviews by pseudo-novelists or "muckraker" journalists who wanted to see their name on the third page of *Midi Libre* . . .

When I told them I would be delighted to describe my days entirely spent packaging scented candles, they flocked to candidates more suitable for tragedy, even if it meant slipping into lies or the absurd.

But, growing older, I've exhausted my reserve of sarcasm and now I settle for rejecting all interview requests without attempting to learn more about the motives of the requesters.

Concerning the manuscript you mentioned, you must already know the importance it held for me. I gave it to Madame Grant the day before my arrest. Perhaps she spoke to you about our conversations in the shadows of chestnut trees . . . But you have it now, and I assume from this that she has shared that part of her past. If you have the occasion to see her again, tell her that our discussions were not in vain and that she inspired a passion for reading in me. That pastime, in fact, saved me from the chronic depression that takes hold of the inmates here like a whelk to its rock.

I remember the young woman who gave it to me very well. I met her in a rehab facility near Montpellier. Like me, she often went to the library in the center of town and we would cross paths regularly when I was there. On a day of weakness, I told her about the impossible love affair I was entangled in at the time and she told me about a book that had had a certain power over her. According to her, it had helped her to emerge from the self-destructive path she had taken after the death of her parents, and she kindly gave it to me when she left. Although it didn't have the same effect on my life, perhaps for others there is still time . . . So tell the author to publish his book. In schools, hospitals, prisons . . . everywhere lost souls are in need of a sign. And if my testimony can contribute to making it better known, don't hesitate. The simple fact of writing these words to you, after all these years, filled me with an intense joy, even if it is tainted with nostalgia.

I wish you every success.

Cordially,

David Aguilhon

P.S. The young woman is named Elvire and I remember that she was Canadian. I think if you contact the Les Collines rehab facility, they'll be able to dig up her contact information for you in the old logs.

LES CHAYETS, AUGUST 27, 2016

Here I am back in the country after the brief trip to see my daughter, Coralie. As soon as I entered her apartment, I handed her my book and then awaited her reaction with a heaviness in the pit of my stomach. When she realized what it was, she started to jump up and down in the hallway calling for Adam, her partner.

The two of them congratulated me as if I had received the Prix Goncourt and they nearly fought each other to read the first pages. My daughter won and shut herself up in their bedroom with the first part. I searched desperately for a subject to broach with my son-in-law, when he himself started a conversation. Although we hadn't ever exchanged more than ten words, Adam spoke to me with conviction about the last novel he'd read . . . This boy is much more interesting than I thought, and the two of us made dinner without waiting for Coralie, who refused to eat before she'd finished.

When she sat at the table, she had tears in her eyes and I was afraid she would bring up the subject of her mother, forcing me to compare the two loves of my life. But I didn't have to lie to her (which I was ready to do if necessary), because she didn't mention it. She asked me questions about the end of the text and I confessed to her that it existed, but that it had been written by an unknown author. I had left that part at the hotel, but she made me promise to bring it the next day. Finally I described the incredible journey taken by my manuscript and I had the joy of seeing the stunned expressions on their faces.

I've always been on good terms with my daughter, probably—I have to say—because I never exercised my right to veto her activities or her desires. Nevertheless, our relationship was tainted with a certain detachment, as if we didn't have enough things in common to be able to penetrate the other's universe. And then my illness cut me off from the rest of the world and our rare time together was filled with clichéd phrases on her part and unbearable silences in place of response.

That night, closing the door to my hotel room, I was struck by the difference between that night and all the others that had come before it. Our exchanges were no longer restrained, they were natural; Coralie asked me questions about my novel in progress and her interest was genuine.

Alone, facing the window that looked out onto a depressing view of a parking lot, I felt my blood bubbling as if I had just been plugged back in to life. In the eyes of my daughter and my son-in-law, I felt myself exist for the first time, and that recognition slowly erased the feeling of being cast aside, which I had lived with for years.

I don't know if you'll understand, Anne-Lise, because you are still in the heat of the action: your children are still your responsibility, your husband is by your side, and you struggle to manage a household while working a demanding job. But our years of difference had pushed me into the realm of observers, people who have time and who live without hours or constraints (those of my profession being almost nonexistent since I am able to work from home).

In that state, sometimes we forget that we are still alive.

And so I return a man transformed; the same in appearance, but with a completely different mindset. Almost as soon as I arrived home, I opened my mail and saw your little note concerning the cancelation of our "trip" to prison. That made me sad, because this new Sylvestre really wanted to turn back time and rub shoulders with a burglar with a heart of gold.

If you have found any other information during my absence, please do share it with me, because I still have a few days of vacation left to take before the end of the year and I am ready to use them to meet new readers.

For the moment, I will plunge back into writing with delight, for I am making quick progress toward the conclusion . . .

Sylvestre

from William to Maggy

Dear Maggy,

I'm ashamed that I didn't write to you earlier, even if I know that your independence makes you immune to my mood swings. Your letter brought my smile back and I had to restrain myself from jumping on an airplane for Finistère to enjoy the calming effect of the ocean spray in your company.

Last night, while I was walking along the Thames, I lost myself in the memory of our meeting in that pub that you found so charming. I remember every detail of our lunch because that was a timeless moment, like the time we spent in Brittany or Lozère.

And of course, this morning, I woke up too early.

The air was charged with that morning pollution that fills the city when there are several hot days in a row and I decided to clean my London apartment. When everything was tidy, its stark character jumped to my eyes. I thought again of my house in Lozère and of your Breton cottage and I understood that this place is lacking the warmth that would make it welcoming.

Something has made me see the world through new eyes. When I was a child, my mother told me that we could tell we were growing older when we changed glasses. Up until I was a teenager, I believed she was talking about our sight, which diminishes with age. And then one day, when she saw me spending time with Betty, a classmate, she reminded me that three months earlier, I had called that girl dreadfully annoying.

She smiled and said to me: "So, my son, you've changed glasses . . . Congratulations!"

For a few weeks now, Maggy, I have had new glasses. Thanks to them, I have the courage to look behind me, and I feel it is time to reconnect with the people I love and without whom I can no longer picture my future. I know that you'll understand and that you'll forgive me for not having spoken sooner about this past that holds me back.

I think of you very often and I hope that I accompany you sometimes in your morning strolls along the coastal paths . . . Your fragrance indelibly filled the London streets and the aroma follows me each time I walk through the city.

Tenderly,

William

RUE DES MORILLONS, AUGUST 31, 2016

Dear David,

Thank you for the information you gave me. I've just called Les Collines, but of course the secretary refuses to give me the information over the phone. The only way to obtain Elvire's contact information is to visit the director, and even then, they warned me that she is not in the habit of giving out the information of her residents. But I am counting on the extraordinary nature of my request to persuade her.

Reading your letter, I see you are not aware of the illness that has struck Madame Grant. She has lived for several years in a home that specializes in the treatment of those with Alzheimer's, a half hour away from the place where she lived when you saw her for the last time. It would seem that over the years since you left, her memories were erased bit by bit until she fully succumbed seven years ago.

I met her last month and she had the distant demeanor of a person who moves around in life having forgotten how or why she wound up there. She emerged from her lethargy only one time: when she noticed the manuscript sitting on the table, she uttered your name. Do you know what that means? There are attachments so strong that they survive in our memories as if they were physically imprinted in each cell of our bodies . . .

I don't know what your reaction will be when you read this, but I couldn't leave you in the dark about these facts. Maybe you have suffered from no one sharing updates with you, and that is why. I am basing this on the principle that the reality, as upsetting as it is, is always preferable to the endless questioning caused by our brains with more or less reason.

This information is not the only reason for writing you. I am regularly in contact with her son, William, who will soon ask to meet you. Since I know how rapidly you refuse such requests, I'm asking you to give William Grant's more consideration. I think you will both gain something from speaking about a woman who mattered in your lives.

I seem to be meddling in something that is none of my business (and in fact that's exactly what I'm doing), but for reasons that even I can't explain, I am convinced that this text has a power that's bigger than us and I am trying to keep it going through my small means and my naïve advice.

You should know that since I learned of your existence and of the place where you are, I often think of you. I realized this is the first time that I've met (even if only through words on a page) an individual imprisoned in the wake of such crimes (I mean the burglaries and the holdup). I've only known two people who were charged with a crime, and one of them was given a suspended sentence. Both were businessmen who had dabbled in embezzlement for their professional advantage. I draw a distinction between them and your situation: even if I suspect they stole larger sums than you did, they know nothing of the terror one feels walking into a bank with a gun in their hand. They put their signatures on illegal certificates, or authorized money withdrawals from accounts that didn't belong to them; but the risks that they took posed no threat to their physical well-being.

Up until today, I wouldn't have been able to imagine writing letters back and forth with a man who had committed violent theft. But William read me a few excerpts from your letters that he found at his mother's house and I realized I am more sympathetic to your story than to those other two people I mentioned.

The truth is that despite the wrongdoings you are guilty of, I'm sorry that we weren't able to meet, and I am certain it could have marked the beginning of a friendship. If this feeling is shared, don't hesitate to write to me; I will happily respond. I know that you still have a year left behind bars. It might take that long for me to recount for you all the adventures associated with this book that led me to contacting you. You will be surprised by all the twists and turns.

I hope you have the best day possible (meaning: when bars deprive us of contact with nature and our only occupation is packaging scented candles).

Warm regards,

Anne-Lise Briard

P.S. They say there will be one more day of this heat wave . . . do you have air-conditioned rooms in prison? If not, how cruel to have you wrap up candles in this temperature!

P.P.S. Have you thought of writing a novel about your life? If so, don't hesitate to keep me updated—I know editors who might be interested. In fact, I even know publishing houses that could publish a lovely book on scented candles for the year-end festivities . . .

from Maggy to William

Dear William,

Yesterday I went for a three-hour walk along the water and you can be glad I did. If I hadn't forced myself to do so, I would have responded to you right away and you would have seen what an angry woman is capable of writing!

You know nothing about my desire for independence or the care I can feel for people with whom I correspond, but you will learn today that I loathe lies and withholding of information. Your letter is perhaps exemplary in England, but I am past the age of relishing your "tenderly" when you inform me that you are going to reconnect with your past, which no doubt includes a woman (don't tell me there are several!) and one or two children . . . When we reach the half-century mark, we all have a past that we drag behind us with more or less regret, but I believe we must remain honest and not allow ourselves to forget it in one moment only to then use it as protection the next moment.

I imagine you thought, quite arrogantly, that your natural charm had worked its magic on me, the poor solitary and exiled woman. Think again! I am vaccinated against the beauty and cheap compliments of men, and the distance you excuse yourself for taking without much tact will not disrupt my walks, nor my five o'clock tea . . .

I congratulate you for your big spring cleaning and your new glasses—they must suit you marvelously and will be able to provide your gray irises with the insight that they currently lack. Thanks to them, you will have opened your eyes for another reason than that of seducing your entourage, and I encourage you to continue down that road.

From now on, you will no longer have to hammer me with half-truths or allusions to a tenderness that did not exist between us, both because we've known each other for very little time and because we know nothing of each other's respective pasts. If we have to see each other again, which would only happen through the intervention of our mutual friend, keep your distance, and be direct about your former or present attachments. You will then gain a sincere and faithful friend.

When I started writing to you, I thought I might tell you about the tragedy that influenced my life choices. But I won't now. That information is no longer relevant to our platonic relationship. You'll note the sharp tone I'm using today. You know, we Bretons are reserved people, with round and supple contours. We are not of a difficult nature, because our regional survival depends on the ability to accept others and their differences. Brittany is a welcoming land, and this fact has been inscribed over time in our genes. Nevertheless, when we feel betrayed or ridiculed, we transform, all our angles come out, more cutting than Ushant rocks. Don't hold this purely hereditary reaction against me.

I'm still your friend, and I wish you the happiness that you deserve.

Warm regards,

Maggy

AVENUE DU MOULIN-DE-LA-JASSE, SEPTEMBER 5, 2016

Hello Anne-Lise,

Thank you.

Thank you for telling me all of this.

Thank you for rekindling the pain of sentiments that I thought had gone out forever, which allows me to feel alive once again.

You were right, I had no idea about all of Denise's health problems, since I cut off contact with her after my sentence was pronounced. Knowing that I would be imprisoned for a decade, I chose to break the strong bond that had united us. How absurd that my sentencing, the longest I ever received, came at the very moment when I decided to change my life . . . But it was out of the question to drag such a wonderful woman down with me. I knew that she would be ready to leave everything to support me during my struggle. She would have lost her friends and her family only to end up alone in the world, the victim of an impossible love that would have brought her no reward.

I am not a good man. I never was, except perhaps when I was by her side. Despite my desire to keep her close to me, I couldn't bring myself to plunge her into that hell. I decided to preserve her future despite her wishes, and I destroyed all her letters without ever opening a single one. I refused her visits to prison and I prayed for her to find peace with her family, if not with the love that we had lost and which happens only once in life.

After reading your letter, I understood that in my attempt to behave like an honest man, I had caused her misfortune. I am the source of that illness, and so my sacrifice was in vain. *That woman didn't forget me*: five words that drag me into a whirlwind of emotions. The absurd joy of learning that she still thought of me, the pain of knowing that perhaps I could have relieved her suffering, and the depression, of going back to a life that caused nothing but harm to those who crossed my path.

A few days ago I received her son's visit request. I accepted and invited him to come with Denise. Can you please help me and insist that he bring his mother with him? I know that this place is not suited for a woman who has already suffered so much, but I think that her illness will be able to protect her from the negative influence that a prison exerts over sensitive souls. And if it's true that our love has survived, perhaps it can give her the strength to reconnect with our world? I'm dreaming. I'm dreaming and I'm fully aware of it. I would just like to finally do something good and preserve the memory for the day when I leave.

While I'm waiting for my release from prison (which might be early because of my age and a few health concerns), I would be delighted to continue writing to you if the idea of corresponding with a criminal doesn't bother you.

On this note, I have to tell you the truth, at risk of steering your inventiveness to less romantic roads. I am just a thief, Anne-Lise; I never entered a jewelry store with a gun in my hand and I never had to use this kind of aggression. If that were the case, I would have received a heavier sentence each time over the years.

I belonged to a vulgar gang who broke into people's houses and we got our adrenaline rushes from the fear of getting caught when we broke into abandoned villas or when we neutralized, with more or less skill, the alarm systems of small bank offices. Fortunately, we were never confronted by people defending their possessions, because I don't know how I would have reacted in that situation. Today I can tell myself that deep down in me remained a baseline of humanity that would have kept me from hurting another human for money. I believe it. I can never be certain of it.

For that reason more than any other, I will never write a book about my exploits. I would feel as though I were embellishing acts that had nothing heroic about them and were guided solely by the lure of profit.

Best wishes,

David Aguilhon

from Anne-Lise to Maggy

RUE DES MORILLONS, SEPTEMBER 6, 2016

My dear Maggy,

I just received a short note from William. He thanked me for intervening in his favor regarding David Aguilhon, who he will soon meet at the Villeneuve-lès-Maguelone prison.

Guess what? He wants to organize a Christmas party in Lozère! Even Julian doesn't seem opposed to the idea when he sees the joy it brings his beloved daughter . . . And you? What do you think?

We will have an opportunity to talk about all of that soon because I think I should come visit you this weekend. I don't work Monday the 12th or Tuesday the 13th of September, so I could stay four or five days with you. That time will allow us to plan our trip to Belgium and give us a nice break. You know that this is a very busy time at the office, and with age, my neurons require recuperation time after each task. I am aware that by taking breaks I leave the path open for Bastien and his team, but I'm tired. Our nine-year age gap creates a serious rift between our ways of working, and I hate his method just as much as he loathes mine.

So that you'll understand how we've reached the point of no

return, I have to tell you about the incident that shook up the office yesterday morning. For the millionth time, Julian had spent the morning listing off the advantages of me staying at home (he must dream of a partner who cooks him breakfast before he leaves for the office). He doesn't understand that I complain about the pressure I face at the office to then attach myself to my job as to a life preserver. Anyway, I was still furious when I woke up Monday morning and I burned his toast before leaving (inadvertently, I assure you, but his housewife fantasies must have evaporated when he bit into the char).

As soon as I walk into the office, I find out that Bastien has moved up the meeting by one hour because of an urgent trip to Geneva. So there I am, walking into the big room, all eyes on me and the mocking air of my cousin who is surprised that I didn't receive his message (sent to my professional e-mail at eleven-thirty the night before!). With that, he grabs his cell phone, turns around sighing toward the minute taker, and invites him to share with me the decisions that I missed! I responded that not knowing the gossip of the other departments would not stop me from working efficiently this week. Of course, he acted as though he hadn't heard me and continued to smile at his phone screen. I don't know why, but my mind went to his coffee, that Guatemala Antigua that he keeps talking about and that he buys every morning at Starbucks with the sole aim of seeming hip. I walked up to him, I took his new iPhone from his hands, and I plunged it giddily into the bottom of his XXL cup . . . Everyone present stood there with their mouths gaping. I left with as much dignity as possible, followed by Ingrid, my assistant, who I could hear snickering behind me. Bastien's shouts followed me to my office and included the two adjectives "hysterical" and "stark raving mad" which, by the way, are justified given the price of the phone in question. At least he will be forced to endure a few hours without being glued to his Twitter feed!

I know it was a bit much, to speak like my children, and I didn't dare brag about my exploits at home, of course. But I regret nothing. I think that many of our employees rather enjoyed my gesture even if they would never admit it.

And so I need to distance myself from my mailbox and from my phone for a while. In fact I'm awaiting a call from the director of the center in Montpellier where David found the manuscript. You can imagine how anxious I am when I check my voicemail at all hours of the day . . .

Anyway, a break is clearly necessary . . .

In anticipation of your invitation (forced, I know), I am already packing my suitcase and I await your confirmation via telephone (or a call from Agatha if it's too much to ask).

Kisses,

Lisou

P.S. While I'm thinking of it: Katia is in the same class as her friends! I apparently could have been spared from the back-to-school crisis, as I caught whisperings of a certain Yann who sits right in front of her. With a first name like that, I fear the worst. Breton characters can be just as twisted as the trees that weather the storms from the west, and that doesn't mean anything good for my daughter . . .

from Anne-Lise to Sylvestre

Dear Sylvestre,

I am writing to you because it is Wednesday . . . This might seem surprising, but this day is the most peaceful of all for me.

When my children were young, I was in the habit of organizing my schedule in order to leave work in the middle of the week. Like many women, I filled this day with all the tasks associated with the fortune of being the mother of a family: doctor's appointments, gymnastics classes, music lessons, birthday parties, and more. It turns out that my children grew up and I choose to ignore this fact. During the school term (and like all good mothers, I welcome the return of classes), the entire household leaves on Wednesday morning. So I feel something close to ecstasy finding myself with all of this solitary free time. I can devote myself to the sin of listening to music or reading without any interruption during this four-hour period. Oh yes, dear Sylvestre, this pleasure is limited since my daughter comes home from high school at noon and fills the space with repeated attacks aimed at her professors before reorganizing the entire French school system in her own fashion.

Be that as it may, here I am in the eye of the cyclone, and I'm taking advantage of this calm to share my latest inquiries with you. First: Do you think a woman could be the author of the end of your book? Second: Is it all right for me to contact the director of the nursing home again if she continues to ignore me?

I was very clear with her secretary. She insisted on the confidential nature of this information and I had to promise to wait for the director to contact me before bothering her again. What if she's hung me out to dry?

You know that patience is not my best quality: so I have decided to go to Maggy's for a few days to clear my head. For the sake of total honesty, I confess that I am also going there to check on my best friend's well-being. Do you remember how we both joked last month about the attraction between her and our host? I was wrong. Maggy is definitely closed off to love affairs. She just called me from the hotel to confirm that she is expecting me and told me that she will be spending Christmas on the island of Guernsey and so cannot come to Lozère . . . Since she didn't mention William once in those fifteen minutes, it seems like we can forget about that fling!

I am counting at least on your presence at Belle Poelle for the New Year. I would be delighted to introduce you to my husband as well as to my son who, urged by his sister, will join us for the New Year's party.

That's it for the Wednesday report, dear Sylvestre. I'm waiting for your advice with impatience. While I'm gone, I've left my daughter in charge of answering the phone and she has instructions to give your number to the director of the center in Montpellier if she calls. I will be unreachable for several days since cell phones and other means of communication are strictly forbidden at Maggy's. So please, turn off your answering machine and pick up your calls!

Looking forward to your response,

Anne-Lise

P.S. For anything urgent regarding our search, you can always call the Beau Rivage Hotel. Ask for Agathe, who is up to speed about everything and will get in touch with me . . .

from William to Maggy

Maggy,

I found your letter last night when I returned from London and I spent the evening and a large part of the night pacing back and forth in my living room. Fortunately, the English courtesy that you reproached me for obliged me to take off my shoes so as not to disturb the sleep of my neighbors. That way I could freely trample both the softness of my carpet and the severity of your words.

Since I no longer had access to the letter that made you so angry, I had to search for how I could have hurt you so much by studying the list of your accusations. If I spoke of your desire for independence, it was not at all a criticism, but rather a limitless admiration for the life that you lead. I beg you to excuse my clumsiness for deforming the meaning of my words. I don't typically write in French to people dear to me, so perhaps you can forgive me for my poor turns of phrase.

In regard to your comment about the number of wives and children, I can answer you honestly. I was only married once (but if you want me to confess, I have in fact been with other women). Her name was Moïra . . . she passed away in 2008. We had a daughter,

Laura, who now lives with her grandparents and refuses to see me. I don't know if I should tell you any more, but if you would like, you can ask Anne-Lise, who knows all about my past. I don't think I deserved such judgment by keeping quiet about a painful life, but it's true that I was afraid of disappointing you by revealing to you the parts of my past that I am not so proud of.

In that regard, perhaps I do deserve the grief that you gave me.

However, it isn't fair to be angry with me for trying to win you over you when I always felt deprived of affection when we spent time together! I never wanted to disrupt your strolls or your five o'clock tea through the simple fact of my existence or through how much I care about you. If I let slip a sign of contentment, it was that hope you stirred in me by welcoming me into your refuge that you had said was closed to all. How can you so easily neglect the lovely moments we shared in London and in Brittany? What happened to that natural and obvious connection? And our walk back from Roscoff, at night, strolling along the coast from one lighthouse to another, was it nothing but an illusion?

I'm reading your words over and over and I don't understand anything, Maggy, especially not your accusation about my lies or my withholding of the truth. I won't offend you by saying that I never lie, but I can assure you that in your presence I never said anything that wasn't rigorously exact or truly felt. Like that "tenderly" which so irritated you and which escaped from me, it's a fact, revealing the attachment I feel for you that I should have kept to myself if I'm to believe your bitterness.

To finish this plea (and this term, which is not premeditated, testifies to the brutality of your accusations), I must explain that the new glasses I'm wearing (which you brutally removed from my head) were nothing but a projection of what my future could have been had you shared my feelings. I will remove them now, since it's clear that you want me to. So feel free to join in any future reunions we might organize in Lozère without fearing the least demonstration of affection on my part.

William

P.S. You didn't deem it useful to share your own secrets with me. So be it. In your case, it's simply a matter of contempt for me and not a matter of not wanting to share with me . . .

P.P.S. I just bought some stamps and was struck by the front page of the newspapers. I know your passion for photography and it reminded me of our conversations about the snapshots celebrating a dramatic birthday that no one would forget. I hate the outpouring of media that transforms us into voyeurs of individual tragedies. However, I couldn't take my eyes off of one of the photos. It depicted a man, alone, the morning of the disaster. He was among the wreckage. His hands were in his pockets and nothing in his expression evoked the horror he had just witnessed. He could have been cut out and placed, in the same position, in front of a magnificent seaside landscape. And so you see, Maggy, that image unsettled me.

from Sylvestre to Anne-Lise

LES CHAYETS, SEPTEMBER 12, 2016

For the first time, I'm the one leading the dance, and I'm proud of it. While you take advantage of the sea air to clear your head (and believe me, it can only be good for you, I'll tell you why later), I've just received a call from Madame Cartier, the director of the rehabilitation center outside of Montpellier.

She refused to give me the name or the contact information of the famous Elvire, whom David met in 1994 in her establishment, over the phone. When I tried to explain my request, she cut me off point-blank, arguing that she was not paid to discuss novels during her work hours! Quite unexpectedly, I insisted, and offered to go to the South to tell her about my situation in person. She agreed to meet with me, reserving the right to help or not depending on what I told her.

I am going to figure this out very quickly because I leave tomorrow for Montpellier. I have a five o'clock meeting and I am more determined than ever.

You haven't said anything (and for good reason!), but I'd like to think that you are impressed by how easily I've resumed your mission. Here I am prepared to leave northern Île-de-France, where

I had retreated from the world, to meet a stranger in the deep South and to convince her to break the fundamental rule of confidentiality. I am going to use all my skills of persuasion (it's too bad that I don't possess the charm of our English friend) to make her tell me the story.

So that's the next step in this adventure, dear Anne-Lise, and please, don't abuse poor Maggy, and avoid any reference to her trip to the Anglo-Norman island. Seriously! Where did your legendary understanding of the female mind fly off to? The choice of that quasi-British destination doesn't seem surprising to you? I will let you reflect on all this, and we will discuss it as soon as I'm back from the South. In the meantime, please, don't meddle too much in the matters of Maggy's heart and for once, please, trust me!

More very soon, to introduce you to our Waldo, whom I will deliver on a platter,

Sylvestre

RUE DES MORILLONS, SEPTEMBER 14, 2016

Dear Sylvestre,

This weekend in Brittany rejuvenated me. I was so happy to rediscover our carefree teenage habits at our age! Over the course of those four days, we imagined our ideal world as we used to do thirty years ago. We fell back into our hysterical fits of laughter and forgot our daily worries. Of course, we spoke a great deal of your manuscript. We imagined you at twenty years old, in love to the point of making impassioned declarations, and we were in agreement on one thing: we would have swooned over the dark, handsome stranger you must have been at the time. I don't know what you would have done with two teenage groupies hanging on your coattails, but this belated declaration will warm your heart, I have no doubt! If you go to Brittany one day, ask Maggy to show you her photo albums; you will see how irresistible we were thirty years ago . . .

This afternoon, as soon as I got back, I called you and had to have a conversation with your answering machine . . . which you were supposed to have unplugged. After I opened my mail I realized you had left for the South of France. I am very proud of the way you've taken the reins and I'm impatiently waiting for the story of your progress. If you wish to replace me in this quest, at least do it with magnanimity and tell me everything.

On that note, you should know that your (understandable!) fears concerning my lack of insight into the female mind are unfounded: I refused to interrogate Maggy on the subject of her love affairs. It's true, that choice of an English-language destination surprised me, but William cannot be the reason: we will all be in the Lozère house on that date (by the way, Katia has already set aside a few fantasy novels for you).

To tell you the truth, I get the feeling that Maggy is hiding something from me. Even when we were having fun these past few days, I saw worry in her eyes, a tiny grain of sand that partially veiled her sparkle. Have you noticed how obtuse we can be when we try to understand the people that we love? It's almost as if our understanding was handicapped by too much proximity, like how our sight becomes blurry when we look at an object from too close. Your stance will allow you to see things more clearly. Now that I've admitted you understand her better, I'm waiting for your analysis with great impatience.

Anne-Lise

P.S. Don't underestimate yourself, my dear Sylvestre. I promise you that the somber and tormented air you like to put on in all circumstances grants you quite a bit of charm . . . But I imagine you already knew that, didn't you?

RUE DES MORILLONS, SEPTEMBER 15, 2016

Dear Maggy,

I don't understand the message you left on my house answering machine at all. Remember that I have a cell phone and I've given you the number three times: the point of this technological innovation is in fact to be reachable when we are not at home!

What is going on? And what was so urgent that you had to go to Agathe's to use a device that you still have not mastered? Although your tirade was cut off before the end, I grasped the most important thing: you are angry that I knew information about William that I hid from you. If I know parts of his past that you don't, it's probably because I made the effort to ask him questions, so don't be mad at me for my silence regarding facts about which you never expressed interest! And if you want to know more, you will have to stop acting indifferent. On that note, I refuse from now on to respond to your questions in writing. Since you are capable of calling to blame me, you will have to repeat the exploit to feed your curiosity.

I will stop my critiques here, which, of course, are only teasing. Your message did not bother me, it frightened me. The trembling voice I heard didn't match the cheerful friend I left yesterday morning in Brittany. Although I sensed during my stay that something was worrying you, it seemed that I underestimated its importance, and that blindness is not worthy of a friend. So please, Maggy, call me back as soon as you can and I will tell you anything you'd like in order to ease both your pain and your anger.

Your friend, who is still here despite your anger.

Big kisses,

Lisou

P.S. You won't believe it, but Sylvestre left for Montpellier to meet the director of the center I contacted! Soon our misanthropic hermit will become more sociable than a politician in need of votes . . . I have to say that such a sudden transformation makes me a bit nervous. Don't you think that man has a bit of Dr. Jekyll and Mr. Hyde in him?

LES CHAYETS, SEPTEMBER 15, 2016

I returned yesterday and it's my turn to give you a report of the events.

I didn't sleep a wink Monday night, I was so excited at the idea of nearing our goal. I paced in circles and reread the end of the manuscript, asking myself if those lines could have been written by a woman.

Unfortunately I still know nothing about that today . . .

On Tuesday I left very early and was in Montpellier by one o'clock (don't mock my "SNCF timetable" style, you're the one who asked for all the details). I killed time in a café a bit farther down the street. I ate a sandwich, which I hadn't done since I was working in Paris, and I struck up a conversation with the waitress. Perhaps she thought I was a future resident (my tormented air must be marvelously suited for that kind of place), since she willingly described for me the life of the sick, the kindness of the doctors, and the beauty of the garden (she must have worked for a tourist office once). She described a comforting place, and if the term appeared curious to me at the time, it's exactly what came to mind two hours later when I was standing at the front desk. Of course, I was early:

I thought this would show my determination, and before sitting down in the waiting room, I reminded the secretary that I had come from far away for this meeting.

You would have liked Madame Cartier, the Director. The capital letter is intentional. Opposite her, any normally constituted individual would feel inferior: she is as tall as me with broader shoulders. Her voice is very deep, almost masculine, and her eyes penetrate you so deeply that before she even opens her mouth, you are ready to confess all the sins you've committed since you were four years old . . . However, despite this intimidating presence, she makes you feel comfortable and makes you wish she were your best friend.

We walked through the garden and she showed me the center as if I were thinking of staying there . . . For you to understand who we're dealing with, I will tell you an anecdote. While we were talking about the surrounding trees (you know that's a subject I never tire of), I saw her face transform for a fraction of a second. By the time I turned my head to follow her gaze, she had taken off in an Olympic sprint to reach a resident who was sobbing on a bench. I then saw her get down on her knees at the feet of this young woman and grab her hands, speaking in a low voice. Then she whispered a few words in her ear and took out a tissue from her pocket to dry her cheeks. When she came back to me, she had regained all her spirit, and the ailing woman, walking away toward the building, seemed relieved. You see, Anne-Lise, in this world there are individuals who exist who make us feel very small, literally and metaphorically.

Beneath that kindness, I sensed an unstoppable firmness. I was right. I had to battle for a good part of the afternoon to achieve my goal: for Madame Cartier to call Elvire and give her my contact information (since she refused on principle to give me Elvire's number). Despite the resolution I had hoped for in my last letter, I accepted this solution good-naturedly. Sometimes we cross paths with people we don't want to disappoint at any price, and Madame Cartier is one of them . . .

After I left the center I visited the area nearby before going back to my hotel. I was more excited than I had been since the beginning of this adventure. I felt I was close to meeting the person who had been stuck in my mind and had finished my book. Having that intimacy with a stranger must be similar to what having an organ transplant feels like. Someone gave me a part of them so that I could come back to life . . .

The next morning, my phone rang at eight A.M. on the dot and Madame Cartier announced that she had communicated my request to the party in question. It turns out Elvire lives in Canada and would be happy to speak with the author of a text that she has never forgotten. She is very busy but promised to write to me in the coming days. And you will never guess where Elvire lives . . . in Montreal! How about that coincidence? Could it be possible that I crossed paths with this woman last month while I was wandering the Quebecois streets?

So there you have it, the report of my trip to the South. I would have liked to come back with more concrete news to impress you with, but tonight I feel the joy of having met someone remarkable. And, of course, now it's my turn to jump on my mailman friend as soon as he approaches my mailbox, open to the four winds . . .

Sylvestre

P.S. I want to organize a big reunion at the end of our journey, with all the people who have held my manuscript between their hands. I am going to start saving up to be able to pay for the travel costs in case Waldo lives in New Zealand. What do you think of this crazy idea?

from Elvire Lheureux to Sylvestre Fahmer

RUE DICKSON, MONTREAL, SEPTEMBER 17, 2016

Dear Monsieur Fahmer,

I know that my accent makes any phone conversation challenging, so I have chosen to write to you. I don't have the pleasure of knowing you, but Madame Cartier told me that you wanted to know how David came to be in possession of your novel over twenty years ago. I remember him very well. In that type of establishment, the exchanges we have with the other residents are intense, even if they never survive the return to normal life. Between the walls of the center, we forget everything of the exterior. We are as though ejected from the world. That rupture allows us to observe ourselves, without distraction, and to accept what we have become. The reflection that the other residents provide us is our only mirror and we cannot take our eyes off of their features. Each face-to-face meeting brings with it an introspection that leaves us disadvantaged, inept, incoherent. To avoid depression unfurling its opaque blanket over us, there's only one solution: the library.

I am interested in books; certainly through family tradition, but also because I like to write. That activity allowed me to hang on, at a time when my circumstances pushed me to despair.

For you to understand better, I have to tell you more about my situation. I didn't know my father, but I was raised by a stepfather who fulfilled the role to perfection. Unfortunately, a car accident took him from me when I was only thirteen years old. We had hardly buried him when I was placed in a boarding school for rich people's kids. I only went back to the family home during school vacation, and each time I found my mother completely depressed. She suffered, she screamed, she cried; to summarize, she forgot me. Until the day when they called me to say that she had chosen a permanent departure. I was only eighteen years old and I was angry enough to use my inheritance for therapeutic and destructive ends.

So I left school and started organizing parties where the local kids could consume every kind of drug and alcohol that existed on the market. The parties continued at an infernal rhythm, and, to shelter all the partiers who had taken up residence in the house, I decided one morning to clear out the room where my mother had piled up my stepfather's things.

This purging was lifesaving. Anger gave way to sadness. Looking back over all the memories that cluttered up his desk, I cried all the tears I had held back for five years. Would you believe me if I told you that I spent three days locked inside that room? Seventy-two hours during which I ate nothing, just drank (water, what a novelty!), and relieved myself in the adjoining bathroom. It was over the course of this big cleanup of the affairs of the man who had raised me that I found your manuscript. It was still in the original envelope, and the postmark indicated that it came from France. I read it . . .

When I came out of the office, the house had been rid of all its usual parasites. I think the empty fridge and the unpleasantness of the first-floor rooms was the main reason. I took my first shower in days and called my aunt who lived in France and had invited me to her house countless times after my mother's death.

The next day, I took a plane to Montpellier. When my aunt saw the state I was in, she contacted a rehab facility capable of getting me back on my feet. That's how I know Madame Cartier . . . I spent a year under her wing and when I got out, I resumed my studies in the South of France, staying with my aunt and uncle. Now you know the circumstances of my encounter with David. Our friendship was brief because we crossed paths for only two months in the treatment center. But like all relationships begun in distress, it was intense, and I would be happy to know how he's doing.

On Tuesday night when I talked on the phone with Madame Cartier, we had so many things to share that she didn't explain the reason for your search. If you want to know more information, you can call me. We will try to understand each other despite our respective accents (my cell phone number is below).

And if you have the time, can you please send me a copy of your book? I would love to reread it today, now that I'm in a different state of mind, and I would be happy to show it to my daughter.

Thank you,

More soon,

Elvire

RUE DES MORILLONS, SEPTEMBER 18, 2016

Dear William,

I hope you will excuse me for not having written to you earlier. I could blame my son's move, which kept me busy for the end of August, and it would be partly true. But the fact is that I needed some time to digest your words and to know if they changed the image that I had of you.

Of course, my opinion of you has changed. But I can assure you, even after a lot of reflection, that you have not lowered your-self in my esteem. Strangely, I want to say "to the contrary." Your charm and your appeal were hidden, and it's a good thing. In learn-ing more about your past, I saw certain cracks that render a person endearing and lively. If I had a fault to attribute to William Grant as he appeared in his home in July, it would be the excess of perfection in his behavior and physical appearance. Today I can assure you that the scars suit you well. I am happy that you gave up, for a bit, the frivolity you've displayed until now (you tricked us very suc-cessfully!) and I guarantee you that our friendship is solid.

I just received a call from Maggy, who demanded that I tell her more about you. I assumed I had your permission to do so.

In light of the few phrases she choked out, I know that my words were met with sadness. I expected as much. Maggy is habitually a person attentive to others and she will not immediately apologize for having criticized your attitude without seeking to better know you. That turmoil must have knocked her down like a terrible gust of wind. Happily, she is one of those people who get back up after each storm . . .

Now it's my turn to be angry with you for your silence while I've been waiting impatiently to know how your meeting with David went. Did you bring your mother? Did she react when seeing that man who was so important in her life? So many invasive questions, but I know you will not be mad at me for asking them.

Of course, we can talk about all of this at Christmas, but please, between two planes or over the course of a very long flight, pick up your pen and tell me what you know already!

Assuring you of my indefectible affection,

Warmly,

Anne-Lise

P.S. I heard it's eighty degrees in London! Are you walking along the banks of the Thames to try to soak up some of the briskness of the water? It's the same temperature in Paris and it's difficult to go from the air-conditioning of the office to the sweltering heat as soon as we've walked out the door . . .

from Maggy to William

Dear William,

I've made a serious mistake.

You see, for the past few years, I've banished all modern communication from my daily life, resolutely rejecting the rapidity of action and reaction that we impose on this new century. I chose to live on the margin of that mission to make time profitable. That's why I only speak with my friends by letter, hoping to give more value to the phrases that will linger after me.

I was wrong.

The words that I wrote have no more weight than those that spring up without restraint, and most importantly, they don't get any better the more I think about them. I didn't keep a copy of my most recent letter to you, but unfortunately, I happen to have an excellent memory. For that reason, I would have preferred that it be destroyed in the mail, or carried off by a tornado. I had no right to get so angry. If my criticisms seemed unfair to you, it's surely because I cared more for you than I wanted to admit and the mention of memories I was excluded from hurt me. I know the power of the past and I know the influence the dead have on our choices.

Thirteen years ago, I was a lawyer in Paris. I was respected by my colleagues and I had a bit of notoriety within the capital. I fought to defend those forgotten by our society, those that we accuse of every sin because their appearance testifies to a painful existence that we would rather ignore. When they tell their stories, their lives resemble one another's. They had known abuse, lack of security, attacks of primal racism, from their parents, their employers, their neighbors. And like we all do, one day, they had made a mistake. Their suffering had pushed them to strike, to verbally assault a police officer, their anger had led them to steal a car, their fear had led them to drink one too many. When I crossed their path, I went out of my way to grant them absolution. That word is purposeful. I was a lawyer the way one is a priest: with faith.

I was happy. I gave my clients a second chance, and I experienced the same thing in my private life. Completely foolishly, I was in love. So much so that despite my thirty-seven years, I had just decided to have a baby. Me. The woman defiant of all conformity, the one who had always put her freedom before her life . . .

On that day, we had an appointment at the hospital for an ultrasound. We were in the car laughing and coming up with ideas for the name of our future child and I can still tell you the songs that played on the radio. I had just suggested Cunégonde, watching for the reaction on the face of the man that I loved, when I saw it contort. Not because of the name, but because a car was heading for us, going the wrong direction.

What happened next is hazy. I don't know how to untangle the truthful part from the shadowy zone that I created after the fact. My first memories are from the next day, when they told me Richard was dead. The child, still awaiting its name, had not been able to withstand such a brutal accident and she left me, too. In the moment, the miscarriage seemed like a deliverance; I wouldn't have been able to give life to replace the one that had just been taken from me.

It took me six months to reintegrate into the world of the living, begrudgingly. I started working again. Everyone was nice. They gave me the easiest cases, like the one with the seventeen-year-old who had taken his father's car to drive his girlfriend home. It was only three miles. He had only had one beer. This was confirmed by all the witnesses. The road was slippery. He had lost control of his car. I remember his angel face ravaged by regret and guilt faced with the consequences suffered by the young woman whose car he had crashed into.

I was not touched by his remorse.

No one in my practice knew the circumstances of the accident that had killed my child and my husband. The other driver had also been a young man. He had collided with our car because he'd had too much to drink, and had gotten off without a scratch. And so my associates didn't understood why I took my things and deserted the office without a word of explanation. The next day, I left for Brittany. I opened the shutters to my family home and I set down my suitcase in the bedroom. For two years, I didn't set foot back in Paris.

Anne-Lise sold my apartment and handled all the paperwork, even forging my signature. When she brought the last of my things, she arrived with a job offer. She knew a publishing house that was looking for children's book authors. I refused. And two months later, I sent them the first draft of a children's book.

That's the pathetic story that turned me into the woman with the independence you praise. A woman detached from everything—except, of course, from her past . . .

I owed you this story, William.

During the few days spent here, we lied. We slid into the skin of the people we could have been, the people we might have dreamed of being, in another life. I had no right to judge you. I hope you will forget the harshness of my words and I pray that they didn't bruise you too badly.

In friendship,

Maggy

from David to Anne-Lise

AVENUE DU MOULIN-DE-LA-JASSE, SEPTEMBER 20, 2016

Hello Anne-Lise,

A few days ago, I received a visit from William Grant. He came with his mother. Between his busy schedule and the difficulty of obtaining the visitation authorization, the meeting was no simple matter to organize. But William possesses that rare and precious smile that opens all doors—he gets it from his mother.

Denise didn't say a word, but she stared at me from the second she entered and didn't take her eyes off of me for the entire meeting. When she left, she took my hand and squeezed it intensely. Her son assured me that it was rather exceptional for her to be so attentive and for such a long time. So I will be happy with that reaction and it will brighten the coming days.

Paradoxically, it's been a long time since I've felt such intense solitude. I realized that outside of packaging candles and going to the gym, I do nothing with my days. For the first time, I felt shut in. You must be thinking, it's about time I realize I've spent nearly twelve years of my life behind bars! Is it because of Denise's illness? I realized yesterday that she was perhaps shut inside her oblivion so she could experience the same circumstances as me . . .

Do I seem crazy to you? Probably. That's why I preferred not to say anything about this to William. However, I encouraged him to bring his mother to Lot, to the house where we had been happy, even if only briefly. He was astonished to learn that I had kept the house and that Denise was still the owner. I'm sure he thought that I had taken back this house to have a place to stay between robberies. In fact, I've only returned there one time, when I finished serving my longest sentence, hoping to find a sign of her there. While I've been in prison, I've dreamed that she was spending vacations there, sheltered from the world. But it seems that she never returned after our separation. Her son wrote down the address. I know he'll keep his word and bring Denise there, because he too is praying that a familiar place might manage to free her from her own jail.

That's all the updates that I'm able to give you. Outside, the sky is still blue, but I presume, based on the subdued lighting, that autumn has arrived, and it's the season I dread the most here. It's when I miss taking walks through the big forests in Lozère, the nights spent listening to the wind, and the sound of the bugs cracking beneath our steps . . . Enjoy all of that for me if you return to Belle Poelle.

The hardest thing is not the enclosure of my body, but that of my sight. My eyes are constantly searching for a horizon, for a limit that exists only in nature. The foliage of the trees, the peaks of a mountain, the soft lines of a hill or the curve of an immense sea . . .

Here where I am, there is nowhere I can escape to. Each glance collides with the vertical lines of walls or bars and my field of vision shrinks a little more each day . . .

Best wishes,

David

RUE DES MORILLONS, SEPTEMBER 21, 2016

Dear Sylvestre,

Bravo once again! I have been so happy since your call. What luck that Elvire kept the note that was with the manuscript's package! And a big thanks to her for organizing all the boxes containing her parents' affairs on Saturday. I can imagine how exhausting that must be. I hope she finds that precious envelope and the name of the sender very soon.

If so, perhaps we will discover why a stranger finished your novel after finding it in an airport . . . On that note, I have to tell you the horrible dream I had last night: we found our Waldo's address, we were on our way there, and we arrived in a place invaded by brambles. On the door was a death notice. I woke up suffocating and had to dry the tears I had cried during my sleep. See how much all of this has taken over my mind!

And you, what do you feel, dear Sylvestre, knowing we are approaching the truth? Joy? Anxiety? Was it out of fear that you sent your daughter to get the name we've been waiting on for months? When I think she will probably deliver the identity of Waldo on Saturday night, I get chills!

Please contact me as soon as you know. As you can imagine, I won't be able to sleep waiting for your call. I am not alone—Maggy made me promise to call her at the hotel, where she will be having dinner with Agathe, listening for my call. I am certain that for the first time, she regrets not having a cell phone.

I know that this letter is useless since we spoke yesterday, but I needed to put on paper the happiness I feel reaching the end of the road. I feel like those hikers who set out on a pilgrimage and who know that at the next bend, they will glimpse the end of the journey. I feel equal parts joy and sadness at the idea that a page will turn and our quest will stop.

Still waiting to see whether you were right about Maggy's love life, I have been avoiding any reference to England, to Belgium, but also to Lozère, to gray eyes, to men in general. Soon I will have to specialize in stamp collecting or astrology so I can make small talk. Although stamps might be associated with letters not received and the study of stars could awaken the memory of the skies full of stars we contemplated this summer in Belle Poelle . . .

Hopping up and down awaiting your imminent revelations,

Your accomplice,

Anne-Lise

POINTE DES RENARDS, SEPTEMBER 22, 2016

Dear Lisou,

I'm sorry again for the answering machine message that worried you so much. You know it's difficult for me to have a conversation with a machine. Why was I so aggressive? I have no idea. Perhaps my fifth decade drawing to an end is toying with my mood in addition to my hormones . . .

I apologized to William as well and everything is back in order (I hope so anyway). I think I've forgotten how to be around men. From now on, I'd rather avoid them, because the friendlier they are, the more suspicious I am and the more hostile I get. That's why I needed some time to recover a certain equilibrium after our trip to Lozère.

I know what you think about this and I appreciate that you are keeping it to yourself. No, Richard is not responsible for all this. The image of the ideal man to which I had attached myself after his death doesn't exist anymore. I accepted this a long time ago. Our relationship in that moment had been chipped away by the years and, with time's help, I've become aware of his faults. We even had arguments sometimes, which distanced us from each other. You see, the lesson is learned and internalized . . . even if it's not effective.

So let's let Richard rest in peace and accept the reality: I am just an old woman who has lost the ability to fake the happiness that interactions with men are supposed to cause. I know William understands and will accept my apologies.

Considering this slight mishap, you will be relieved to know I'm not coming for Christmas. You have no need for a killjoy who might just spoil the party with her mood swings! However, I am still delighted at the idea of going with you to Brussels and I will be available on the dates you sent me. I cannot wait to discover the city that so thrilled you and I promise to behave myself and not bite any Belgian during my stay.

On Saturday Agathe and I are planning a real night out (the term "night out" means that I will ditch my hole-riddled sweater and my rabbit-head slippers that, even in a suburban restaurant, might draw a little too much attention to my lack of social skills). We will share a delicious meal accompanied by a good bottle of wine, and we will raise our glasses of Chouchen each time the phone rings. As you can tell, we will be awaiting the so eagerly anticipated news with great joy (Chouchen is the best tranquilizer).

Hugs,

Talk to you Saturday,

Maggy

from Anne-Lise to David

Dear David,

I am happy to hear you accepted William's visit request. I just left another message on his cell phone . . . Since he didn't answer my last three calls, I didn't expect much from the fourth. His silence doesn't worry me. I know his life is in perpetual motion and I imagine that quiet and distance are often necessary to his survival.

On the other hand, I am worried about your fate. Where will you live in a few months, David? Do you dare to confront the memories lurking in that house in Lot?

Maybe it would be better to distance yourself for good from Marseille, which doesn't seem to have had a good influence on your life choices. How will you get by? Is there a retirement pension for thieves? Welfare for criminals?

Please excuse my nosiness once more, but I can't bear the thought that you'll end up on the street when you finally get out of there. Even if we've never met, you are now part of my circle of friends and I would be happy to help if you have any problems when you get out.

And on the subject of meeting, is it possible that you might be able to get authorization to leave for New Year's Eve? We would be delighted to have you join us in Lozère for the celebrations, because we're thinking of organizing a reunion that would bring the grand adventure of this manuscript to an end in a fabulous way. We've almost reached our goal. Soon I'll be able to tell you how the story ends.

I get chills thinking about it.

Who will we discover? Did we dream too big about the end of our journey? Will we be disappointed coming to the end of this saga only to find some nondescript individual who might have forgotten all about this text, or worse, who would not care about it today? Yes, I am afraid. I pray for the conclusion to be worthy of the novel we have come to love because, in the end, only the conclusion grants a work its grandeur and longevity.

In any event, I will keep you up to date on what happens next. You are a link in this chain, David, a chapter of this book . . .

In friendship,

Anne-Lise

P.S. In Paris, we do not smell the fragrance of autumn and I cannot, this year, experience Lozère swathed in the colors of fire, nor hear the bugs cracking underfoot . . . In any event, I am excited to see it in winter. I'm dreaming of a white Christmas, lost in the middle of those forests that you love.

from Sylvestre to Anne-Lise

LES CHAYETS, SEPTEMBER 23, 2016

I broke the unspoken agreement with my mailman and used my phone to talk to one of our friends. I have an excuse, though: William moves from one city to another at lightning speed, and I had to reach him without delay. I'm sending you an excerpt of a letter that he has written to me since then, an excerpt that will prove to you that I had good intentions:

> I've just left Scotland to go back to the United States, but if everything goes well you will meet Laura during the year-end vacation!
>
> Thank you for your help and for the long conversation we had a few days ago on the phone. I decided during the summer to try to speak to my daughter again, and you are the one who convinced me to jump on a plane without hesitating any longer. After understanding that nothing would bring my mother back to this world, I finally admitted that the future was too uncertain and that I shouldn't push important things to tomorrow.
>
> So I left right away for Scotland and arrived for dinner at my in-laws'. I didn't give my mother-in-law the chance to kick

me out; I immediately walked into the dining room to speak directly to Laura, who was looking at me as if she'd just seen a ghost. I spoke for fifteen minutes without anyone interrupting me and I told her everything. My remorse, my fears, my love for her, my sadness confronting my mother's state, and my hope of finding a place in her life again. I even spoke of your book, Sylvestre, and would you believe me if I told you how she reacted? She gave a slight smile, lowered her head as her mother often did, and asked me: "Will you lend it to me?"

I cried.

And you got off easy because if you'd been there, I would have hugged you, despite my British prudishness and your classically French crabbiness . . .

I cannot re-transcribe everything for you. But from that long discussion between father and daughter arose the possibility that Laura might live with him after her A levels and continue her studies in London. William begged me to send my manuscript to his daughter, so I just did. He is counting on this text to convince her to spend Christmas vacation with all of us. I don't know if I'll have the power.

I can't get over that I helped our friend to begin something he's been putting off for so many years. I am happy about it, Anne-Lise, and I hope that the discovery of Waldo will not destroy this new happiness I've felt for the past few months.

Of course, you'll be the first person I call tomorrow night. And

I think soon we'll be able to plan a meeting with the three of us. If we have to go to Canada for it, my daughter will take care of housing and I will pay for your plane ticket.

Everything seems possible in this moment. So, for all of this, I thank you, Anne-Lise.

Talk to you tomorrow on the phone.

Sylvestre

P.S. As passionate about literature as you are, having read so much about human passion, how can you not see how hard our two lovebirds are trying to avoid each other?

And if you want proof, ask yourself about this trip that Maggy is taking at Christmas, whose dates perfectly line up to justify her absence in Lozère! I am willing to bet that she has no reservation in the Anglo-Norman islands! She is just afraid to confront the person who disturbed her solitude. As for William, for the first time since his wife's death, he puts a stop to his perpetual running around and finally finds the strength to stabilize and reconnect with his daughter . . . What do you think of that turnaround?

It's easy to tease them from our position as observers, but would we be any more daring if we were in their place?

from Anne-Lise to Maggy

RUE DES MORILLONS, SEPTEMBER 25, 2016

Hi Maggy!

How are you? Have you heard from William? I haven't. I learned about his most recent travels through Sylvestre. It sounds like he wanted a man's advice before going to Scotland to resume contact with his daughter. Yes, his daughter . . . That's the past he wants to reconnect with in order to move forward in his life.

I'm telling you this even though it's not really my place because you are my best friend. As such, I will also tell you that I can no longer bear watching you lie to yourself so obviously. Open your eyes, Maggy, and face the fact that you might be in love. That would explain your mood swings much more than your hormones, and your obvious avoidance of that man gives you away even more than the attention normally given to him by women.

Richard won't turn over in his grave if you confess your feelings, and if you had died in his place, he wouldn't have waited thirteen years to live his life. That's how men are and I agree with you: they are inconsistent beings that should never be trusted.

Yes, I'm angry too. I'm sorry that I didn't call you last night, but I was counting on Sylvestre's promise and he let me down. How could he have forgotten me while I spent a good part of the night with my cell phone glued to my ear (with the volume at the lowest setting so as not to wake Julian)? At two A.M., I left a message on his voicemail, then a second, then a third. Nothing. At five A.M. I started sending him text messages. Still no response.

I didn't start to insult him until ten A.M. (please note my patience and my restraint) and since then, I've been joyfully compiling a list of all the afflictions I would make him suffer if he were in front of me . . . It's not very productive, I know, but it makes me feel better!

The only person who can give me information about the interview yesterday is that famous Canadian Elvire, who found the manuscript in her stepfather's things, but unfortunately, I don't have her contact information. I even almost called a Coralie Fahmer whose number I found, before I saw on her Facebook page that she has several grandchildren!

I think I have a right to know the end of this saga that I started, don't I? At worst, Elvire's information will have led us to a roadblock or led us back to a deceased person (I hope not; that would be an enormous disappointment for us all). In any case, dead or alive, Waldo should have been revealed to us last night, and nothing justifies Sylvestre keeping their identity a secret . . .

You will understand my frustration when I tell you that at two A.M. I constructed a catastrophic scenario in my head. I imagined a car accident that put Sylvestre in the hospital, a partial amnesia explaining his silence . . . I couldn't get back to sleep and started cleaning my entire house so I could temporarily escape the plans constructed by my nonstop imagination.

Fortunately, a mountain of work awaits me tomorrow at the office and will allow me to avoid a second day of mistreating my husband and children.

More very soon,

Kisses,

Lisou

P.S. Don't get mad at me for being honest about your feelings for William; we're past the age of lying. If you choose to remain in denial, I won't bother you anymore with these thoughts, but if you hesitate, think of those gray eyes that marvelously adorned your Breton living room, that perfectly matched the sea you can see from your window. I know you are still open to arguments concerning your interior decoration, and when all is said and done, do men deserve to be considered any other way?

from William to Maggy

Dear Maggy,

I have finally decided to answer you. If I offend you once again with my words, please erase them immediately or chalk it up to that clumsiness that comes over me when I try to speak to you. More ample excuses would seem insincere and that's the only reason why I'll stop here.

You told me your story as if our two pasts were now on equal footing. That is not the case. Your behavior might be beyond reproach, you might have committed no fault which led to the death of your partner and your child, but I cannot free myself with you. My role in the sadness that destroyed my family makes it nearly impossible to forgive myself.

For a few days now, I've been speaking with my daughter regularly and I am glad she is indulging me after we had remained separated for so many long years. To win her over, I was open with her in a way I wasn't able to be with you, and no doubt the lecture you gave me at the beginning of the month was helpful. But don't worry, I won't take advantage of the happiness I owe in part to you to harass you once more with my feelings.

They are real, but will transform over time into a sincere and loyal friendship.

So you will have nothing to fear if you agree to celebrate the New Year with us, and I am inviting you again to the celebration of Saint-Sylvestre (there will be so many of us that you will be able to avoid me rather easily). Your absence would be harmful to the success of such a celebration and I would consider myself responsible for your decision not to attend. You would intensify my guilt even more and I know that is not what you want. And note how the date is perfect to celebrate our friend!

I've given you my best arguments, Maggy, and I'm impatiently waiting for your response. I would be happy to open my door to you with as much simplicity and kindness as you did for me in Brittany, and this time with no ulterior motive or maneuver to win your attention.

See you very soon I hope,

Warm regards,

William

P.S. I have no words to express what I felt learning about the suffering you've faced. Don't take my silence on the subject to mean that I don't care . . .

WILLYGRANT@GMAIL.COM

MONTREAL, SEPTEMBER 28, 2016

Dear Anne-Lise,

Since I was already in the United States, I went to Montreal as soon as I received your call. I didn't tell you that Sylvestre had given me the contact information for his daughter Coralie because you would have said it was reckless to take this trip. But your distress on the phone and the lack of any professional obligation for the next few days brought me here in search of an explanation for Sylvestre's "disappearance."

On Tuesday I was able to meet Coralie, who told me what she knew. When she went to see Elvire Lheureux (that is the full name of the Canadian woman who gave the book to David), she read the letter that accompanied the package, which was dated January 7, 1987, and signed with just a first name. In her letter, the sender addressed Elvire's stepfather, to whom she says she is "returning the novel." She asks him to forgive her for keeping it for four years and adds that she took advantage of that time to write the ending. Coralie immediately called her father, who cried with joy at the other end of the line when he learned that the end had been reached.

But when she read him the name on the back of the envelope, Sylvestre hung up without a word. Since then, she's had no word from him and of course his phone is going straight to voicemail. No need to tell you that she's very worried.

Back at the hotel, I consulted the Internet and after two hours of research, I flushed out this Claire Laurent-Mallard. She's a French author of detective novels, better known in France under the pseudonym Laurent MacDrall.

This morning, proud of my discoveries, I accompanied Coralie to Elvire's. She told us about her stepfather . . . and that's when it clicked: remember, in Lozère, Sylvestre told us that he had lost his manuscript while he was visiting his friend Achille, who was the editor in chief of a literary magazine. I asked Elvire: her stepfather was named Achille Gauthier! So, the original person it had been addressed to had gotten Sylvestre's manuscript not long after its disappearance in 1983. Why did he send it to this woman without saying a word to Sylvestre?

Only one person can answer this: the woman who goes by Laurent MacDrall. And it's easier for you to contact her.

I'm thinking of going back to London at the end of the week, after I see a former colleague exiled to Quebec and have dinner with Elvire, who is interested in my poker playing and would like to hear a few anecdotes about my most recent tournaments.

In any event, it will be a pleasure to scold Sylvestre (with your help I'm sure) as soon as he reappears.

Hugs,

William

P.S. Don't tell Maggy that we're corresponding by e-mail now; she will lose respect for us.

CLAIRELAURENT@FREE.FR

ROUTE DE COURMAS, SEPTEMBER 30, 2016

Madame Briard,

I am responding to you using this name, since that's the one you used in your letter, but imagine the expression on my editor's face when he noticed your envelope with that heading among the mail he receives for me each day!

I would have given anything to be there at that moment and take a photo. He called me immediately after (at least I hope) and when I swore that I had never met you, he continued to get himself worked up on the other end of the line. I ended up giving him permission to open the envelope and read me what was inside so that he would calm down.

From that point on, my face was frozen in shock! To rediscover a text I thought had disappeared or been abandoned at the back of a closet thirty years ago, and to learn that it had journeyed from hand to hand to eventually arrive in your own: I don't know whether I should laugh or cry! Of course, hearing about a manuscript I had seemingly hidden from my editor launched him into accusations that I refused to respond to for a long time. I promised to explain everything to him once I had contacted you, but I immediately warned him that I had no right to this story, to which I had only brought a modest contribution thirty years ago.

Even if I come off as a bit detached, in reality this novel holds great importance for me. It has a very special place in my heart and I could, even thirty years later, recite passages to you from memory . . . That's why I will come to Paris. You told me you'll be away from October 8th to the 13th, so I'm inviting you to meet me Wednesday the 5th, at noon, in the restaurant whose name is below. It doesn't look like much but the food is very good, and most importantly, it is a nice, calm place for when you want to have a conversation in peace.

I am delighted to read and reread the copy of your letter sent to me as an attachment by my editor. I cannot wait to hear more and to find out your role in this affair.

Looking forward to meeting you,

Yours,

Claire Laurent-Mallard

P.S. The restaurant reservation will be in my name, important to note in case you arrive there first. Of course, I am not informing anyone of our meeting, certainly not my editor. I like him a lot, despite all his faults, and I refuse to be the cause of one of those fainting spells he is so fond of and which he generally blames one of his authors for, thinking that guilt spurs our writing.

ALISE.BRIARD@YAHOO.FR

RUE DES MORILLONS, OCTOBER 1, 2016

Dear William,

I followed your advice and everything is happening very quickly: I have a meeting with Claire Laurent-Mallard on Wednesday. I used my maiden name, which is also, as you know, that of a Parisian publishing house. It goes without saying that this sped up our conversation . . .

Claire told me that this novel holds a special place in her heart. It was after all the beginning of her career, but I cannot help myself from thinking, perhaps foolishly, that there exists a stronger link behind all of this.

You deserve to experience the developing of this adventure at our sides, William, and so I'm inviting you to come to Paris to hear the story from Claire herself. I also invited Maggy (don't worry, I have two guest rooms now that my older son has left to pursue his studies in the country and you can avoid each other, except perhaps in the hallway that leads to the bathroom since it is very narrow, but if necessary, we will establish precise hours of moving about).

To simplify your cohabitation, I lied to my friend. I promised her that she would have no more reason to fear your affection because you had told me that you had been seduced by a certain Elvire, who turned out to be more vulnerable to your charm. Given her change of mood (very noticeable at the other end of the line) and the questions she asked me about her, I am now sure of her feelings. Up to you to see how you will use this information. Nevertheless, allow me to give you a piece of advice: let this doubt linger between you two for a bit and maintain my lie by speaking of Elvire more than necessary. I adore Maggy, but she needs an electroshock to own up to her feelings.

No matter your decision, a room awaits you here. Also, you should know that Claire Laurent-Mallard has just accepted my suggestion that I come with two friends on Wednesday.

Hoping you arrive in time,

Hugs,

Anne-Lise

P.S. In fact, what is your relationship with Elvire? I noticed that you spent time alone and I hope that the lie I constructed to make Maggy jealous has no basis in reality . . .

WILLYGRANT@GMAIL.COM

MONTREAL, OCTOBER 2, 2016

Dear Anne-Lise,

I will be at Roissy Tuesday morning at 8:25 A.M. If that works for you, I will stop at your house first to leave my suitcase (I am thrilled to see you again, as well as Katia and Maggy, and to meet your husband). I will go with you to the restaurant and I thank you for inviting me to meet the author we have been waiting to meet for so long. Thanks also for all that you wrote me. I am happy and it has nothing to do with Elvire.

Kisses,

William

P.S. I have a few meetings to get to in Brussels, so I can make the trip with you to our Belgian capital if you are still taking your trip to Belgium (and of course if Maggy does not get mad).

from Anne-Lise to William

ALISE.BRIARD@YAHOO.FR
RUE DES MORILLONS, OCTOBER 2, 2016

Dear William,

What to say? Can't wait for Tuesday!

However, I won't be at the house to welcome you because I still have to go to the office from time to time . . . if only to annoy my cousin and mark my territory.

But have no fear, Maggy will be waiting for you . . .

See you Tuesday night at the house,

Hugs,

Anne-Lise

RUE DES MORILLONS, OCTOBER 5, 2016

Dear David,

As promised, I will tell you the end of the story that brought us all together. This afternoon, I dined with the long-awaited author (a woman!). Even in my wildest dreams, I couldn't have imagined a more fitting end to this adventure.

I already told you that Sylvestre lost his manuscript in 1983, while he was on a trip to Quebec. While he was passing through, he had planned to leave the first part of his novel in Montreal, with a friend who worked in the literary world. He was hoping to get an impartial opinion (if that exists) on his text before writing the end. Unfortunately, when his plane landed, the bag that contained the text had disappeared, and after a few fruitless searches, Sylvestre abandoned all hope of finding it again. For more than thirty years, he had no idea that an attentive passenger had sent it to his friend. Why didn't the friend tell Sylvestre he had received it? That question remains unanswered for the moment.

On the other hand, we have finally learned the reality hidden behind the novel. In 1982, while Sylvestre was harvesting grapes in Champagne, he fell in love with the daughter of the vineyard owners. That was Claire Laurent-Mallard, the author we met this afternoon. The same summer, Sylvestre met Achille Gauthier, the famous Quebecois, who was staying in one of the guesthouses connected to the farm. The man had moved to France for three months to write a book on French vineyards. Over the course of those days, he got on well with Sylvestre, then became his confidant and the sole witness to the budding love affair.

That came to an end with autumn, when Sylvestre had to return to Paris for university. Aware of their youth and warned of the inconstancy of promises we make at that age, the two lovers decided it was easier not to confront the social differences between their two lives, and never saw each other again. Sylvestre chose to soothe his sadness with writing while Claire believed she had simply been forgotten.

What happened next we learned from Claire herself, who was surprised one day to receive an envelope containing the start of Sylvestre's novel.

Achille probably gave her these pages because he wanted her to be aware of the depth of the young man's feelings. He hoped to reunite the two young people to give their love a second chance. What he didn't know is that, in the meantime, Claire had developed an illness of an uncertain fate (during our meeting, she didn't want to say any more about it and we respected her discretion). Not wanting to reveal the gravity of her state to Sylvestre, she hoped to preserve the manuscript as a memory of their former love. When the doctors gave her a glimpse of a chance at recovery, she took it as a sign and set about writing the ending. At lunch this afternoon, she used these words: "When I wrote the last period, I knew I was cured; I had no need for medical analysis, I felt my blood pumping through my veins once more like the sap of a tree in spring . . ."

In 1987, she received the confirmation of her full recovery and sent the finished text to Achille, thinking he would send it back to Sylvestre . . . But time had passed. She didn't know that a car accident had mowed down Achille, killing him on the spot and preventing him from fulfilling his mission as messenger.

So there you have it, a story as extraordinary as can be. It contains enough plot twists, great passions, and missed opportunities to give rise to a vital work.

There's more. Our Claire has hidden for years behind the pseudonym of Laurent MacDrall, which you must be familiar with if you are a big reader. This afternoon, when William wanted to know whether this discovery would inspire another novel, she responded, with a certain forcefulness, that it was out of the question and that she had written the end, at that time, with the sole aim of moving Sylvestre to return to Champagne. The tragedy is that during all this time, she thought he had received his manuscript but hadn't deemed it a good idea to get back in touch with her. I wouldn't know how to describe her face when she realized that he had only just been reunited with it and that he had remained very attached to it.

Next, we had to tell Claire that Sylvestre had disappeared on the day he learned her identity. She was quiet for the rest of the meal and, before leaving, told us that she knew of two places where he might have chosen to hide. Refusing to reveal any more to us, she asked for a few days to verify her suspicions. She promised to keep us updated and embraced us all.

When she left the restaurant, she had been rejuvenated to such an extent that I thought I saw her skip in the street (perhaps the effect of the champagne). I remember writing to you about those feelings that seem imprinted on each cell of our bodies. I believe the love that bound (and my sixth sense tells me I shouldn't speak in the past tense) Sylvestre and Claire is of the same nature as the love you shared with Denise.

Today, a new couple forms under my roof and, if the protagonists follow their own winding paths before giving in, I can promise you that the outcome is already written somewhere. Strangely, it is only as teenagers that we plunge into love as if we were going to die the next day. The older we get, the more we hem and haw; as if time no longer mattered. Isn't it funny?

If all my predictions turn out to be true, we will have more to celebrate than the new year. But perhaps I am inclined to believe in romance more than the average person because of my profession (I will tell you more about that in person, so I can have the pleasure of seeing you smile when I do).

In the meantime, I am impatiently awaiting Sylvestre's return and the joy of preparing the New Year's festivities when we will finally meet.

Best wishes,

Hugs,

Anne-Lise

from Anne-Lise to Maggy

My dear Maggy,

You will find this letter Thursday, returning home after our marvelous escapade in Belgium. Tonight the words come easily to the page as I hear you humming in the shower a few feet from the walnut desk where I'm writing. How long has it been since your looks, your smiles, your gestures have exuded so much tranquility?

"Not since Richard died" you will respond without hesitation! I will not contradict you, but I know deep down that you have never been so radiant. Yes, even during your time with the man you call the love of your life and from whom you would never dare strip this title because death donned him with a halo he didn't possess in his lifetime . . .

For me, the love of your life is named William. Not only because he's a beautiful person inside and out and because I get along with him as if we were childhood friends, but also because he came into your life when you had found serenity again and you had no need for anyone to support you. That's why this love is perfect. Because it's happening at the right moment of your life, when you're not waiting for anything other than what he has to offer you: happiness in every moment.

I am quickly sealing this envelope before you come out of the bathroom.

Don't ever forget that I love you like a sister,

Lisou

from Anne-Lise to William

RUE DES PIERRES, BRUSSELS, OCTOBER 9, 2016

Dear William,

You were dying to accompany us to Brussels, and even though we begged you, you understood that we needed this time for us women and I appreciate that. Don't worry, during this short trip I will survey Maggy's comings and goings and make sure no Belgian distracts her attention . . .

In all honesty, it's not every day we cross paths with poker players with irresistible gazes, not even in Brussels . . . Maggy is smart enough to have realized this in time and to have made a step toward you before you fell completely under Elvire's powers!

We will confess our lie to her at Christmas, when she meets the Canadian woman . . . Although . . . Perhaps I should instead ask Elvire to play along? That will keep us both from having to confront Maggy's fury when she learns about our dishonesty. That would also guarantee you her constant attention for the entire trip. Believe me, it is adorable to watch you two in the corner feigning an indifference that no one believes and which we all talk about as soon as your backs are turned.

I am happy to learn that Claire found Sylvestre. I will enjoy this weekend more now that I know where they are. I have to stop writing now because the hairdryer in the bathroom has just stopped and I don't want Maggy to know about our secret correspondence!

More very soon,

Your friend,

Anne-Lise

P.S. I've started addressing you formally again. I think I'll keep it up for a bit longer. The courteous "vous" that you don't have in English lends French an inestimable value and superiority in its wording. For that reason, I write more joyously to the people I address formally.

from Claire to Anne-Lise

Dear Anne-Lise,

I am back on my home turf. I spent all my autumns here. Writing. In this attic that I fixed up years ago and where I piled up all the books that mattered. In the distance, there's still a slight haze over the ground that obscures the vines that surround the house. I'm not bothered by it, I already know the colors of the vines when the light penetrates to the heart of the forgotten bunches, and I savor this blur that is synonymous with a big part of my life.

I was twenty when my vision brutally deteriorated. That's how they found the tumor. For several years, I lived without being able to see more than two feet in front of me. People were imprecise silhouettes, recognizable through their gestures or their gaits. I got used to imagining everything I couldn't recognize. Based on scents, colors, contours, the suddenness of movements, or the gentleness of words, I began reinventing the people around me. Then, naturally, I wrote their story. The distance was manageable; just over a foot from the page, I was able to forget my illness.

I was sent Sylvestre's manuscript when I had just been given my sentence. Two days earlier, I would have taken the train and rushed to Paris to find him again. Instead, I confided in Achille, and I begged him to keep quiet about my circumstances. I waited. Things would eventually come to an end, good or bad. When I lost my hair, I stopped going to university and started correspondence courses. In the beginning, my friends came to the house. I had nothing to say to them. The tumor was all I could think about, and it's not a conversation topic for young people who have their lives ahead of them. So I took refuge in my attic and sank into my memories. We think that at twenty years old, we don't have any memories. That's false. I even wonder if they were all already there by that point. I don't think I've had any new ones since. No doubt because of my failing sight, which prevented me from retaining images. Or else I simply forgot. Unless the doctors left a small piece of the tumor attached to my memory. Who knows.

When the illness was at its worst, finishing Sylvestre's text allowed me to keep him by my side. Him alone. I kept the others at a distance. My loved ones were torn apart by fear and guilt. You know, parents always think they're responsible for everything that happens to their child. And so I learned not to speak of death. I learned to live, intensely, the color of the vines and the sweetness of spring. I learned to savor, without restraint, the violence of the wind that snakes between the vines and whistles when colliding with the stalks. I learned to love men and their strength, their weaknesses too, in every moment. I spoke less about the uncertain tomorrows and spoke of more distant futures.

I finished Sylvestre's novel. It took me four years. The morning

I wrote the last word, looking outside, the vines seemed more alive. I knew that I was cured. As soon as the medical results confirmed my remission, I wrote to Sylvestre's former landlady and got his address. Then I rushed there. I waited several hours at the bottom of his building, our book in my hand. He arrived. On his arm was a young and very beautiful woman. I hid in a café. I hadn't thought for a single second about that possibility. I had put the last few years in parentheses and I was astonished to find that Sylvestre had continued to live. I returned to Courmas and sent the manuscript back to Achille. I waited. I hoped. I hoped to pick life back up where it had been cut off. I hoped that after reading my ending, Sylvestre would ditch the young woman and come back to Champagne.

From the attic window, the road is visible in the distance. So for the first time I grabbed those glasses I always refused to wear to bring the horizon closer. I kept watch. I kept watch for him over the course of writing three novels: eight hundred and ten days to be exact. And then I stopped waiting. And living, I think. I sought an editor and I chose to submerge myself into the lives of others.

Of course, I met men; I even got married, once. After my parents' deaths, I started to direct the vineyard more remotely, between periods of writing and a few publicity tours in the capital. Fortunately, the personnel do very well without me and only consult me to give me the illusion that I still own this land. I didn't have any children and the people who work here wish I had. I know. But one does not bear life when the word "relapse" haunts the beginning of every migraine. No, we simply put our glasses on the nightstand and concentrate on what is distinct, near. The present moment.

What I'm telling you today, Anne-Lise, I told Sylvestre a few days ago. But not everything. No. I didn't mention the pain of his silence. I didn't mention my anger after my trip to Paris. I didn't mention my fear, either. It's too soon. That's why I'm telling you all this. Because we never know if we'll have the chance to go all the way through with our confession and it's reassuring to know that someone knows, somewhere, and that this person will be able to carry on the memory—as books do.

As I write to you, I have a smile on my face. I can talk about my death because I am no longer afraid. My life begins again and I see it in a thousand ways according to the light of day or the dark nuances of night. Does everyone do that? Do you, too, amuse yourself predicting a hypothetical future, recasting the roles of the people around you? It's so new for me . . .

Sylvestre told me what you've done. How far you went for a story that was not your own. He doesn't understand. I do. I know that a story can monopolize our summers and our autumns. I know that a novel can transport us far, penetrate and transform us forevermore. I know that characters on paper can modify our memories and remain forever at our sides.

I wish you a very good night,

Claire

from Sylvestre to Anne-Lise

BEAU RIVAGE HOTEL, LE CONQUET, OCTOBER 13, 2016

Anne-Lise, nearly six months ago, we wrote to each other for the first time . . . and I thank you for having sent me this manuscript lost in the drawer of a nightstand. This piece of furniture that reunited us, I've caressed it countless times over the course of these last twenty days.

On September 24th, when my daughter said the name Claire, it was total chaos. It was impossible for me to react because the emotions flooded too quickly for me to choose just one. So I came to the tip of this unfamiliar peninsula, almost at the edge of the void, here where everything began, to take stock of the situation and allow this unfurling to gently wash over me.

I hadn't picked up on Claire's scent. And yet, all the signs were there. She alone could be generous enough to draw a flattering portrait of me as a young man, setting aside my cowardice of the time. Did I dream of finding her at the end of the road? I don't know. But at the idea of seeing her again and confronting her judgment, I fled. I came to this hotel whose card you gave me and I checked in under a false name. Then I walked . . . The day after my arrival, I had to jump behind some ferns to avoid Maggy, who

I glimpsed at the bend of a path. I hope she won't be mad at me when she finds out. She understands the need for solitude better than anyone.

During those days, I followed the wanderings of my mind with my steps. I retraced the path of that imperfect man who had left his land the day of his eighteenth birthday because he had felt hemmed in. At that age, we don't realize that each step that takes us farther away makes us into a stranger. We don't leave the land that gave birth to us to take root elsewhere.

I think back to that brilliant scholar, so full of pride, who would send word to his family of his successes without ever stepping foot back in the country. He thought he would elicit envy and only fostered pity. Over there, no one dreamed of the capital, no one would have traded the tiniest parcel of land or even the tiniest gray pebble for a diploma or a bank account. That man, Anne-Lise, built his life nevertheless. He believed that a house without a foundation could protect him from torment. He was wrong. The main characteristic of these dwellings is that they are at the mercy of every hurricane, every storm, every gust of wind. So his life was at the mercy of that precariousness. He existed on the surface of life without ever reaching the depths. One summer, he met a rooted woman. She was so similar to him. But unlike him, she knew what was important. She refused to leave her vines and her past. So, he made her pay for that loyalty. He left her without a second thought, without realizing her shadow would loom over him for decades.

One week ago, returning to the hotel, I noticed a silhouette at the front desk. The woman had her back to me. She was playing with her rings and tilting her head in a gesture I would have recognized anywhere. And it was all clear once again. Sufficiently clear in any case for me to walk toward her without hesitation and face her.

She turned around and smiled at me as if we had seen each other the day before.

Do I sound like a teenager? Believe me, I'm aware and I'm not at all ashamed. Claire and I spoke the entire night and for the days that followed until she left again for an obligation in Paris. But during those three days, walking at her side, I no longer knew where I was. Nor when. We roamed the Champagne vineyards and I was astonished at the wrinkles on my hands when I extended my arm to show her the countryside. In my head, I was twenty years old . . .

A FEW HOURS LATER . . .

I was interrupted by Maggy. She just got back from Brussels and found out I was staying a stone's throw from her home (now I know the recipients of Claire's words) . . . She invited me to her place. I confessed to her that the conclusion to our saga had upended my life. Suddenly, I was enchanted by the idea that I had lived only for this moment. That a superior destiny had guided me to this specific day when I would see the love of my youth again.

Maggy laughed at that idea and dragged me to the edge of the peninsula. The wind was blowing and we had to shout to hear each other. Faced with that unbounded nature, which will survive us for a long time, I understood what she was trying to tell me: in one hundred years, no one will worry about my life or the paths I could have taken. Armed with that certainty, I have no more fear.

So to begin, I will rewrite this story. Without Claire. And I will send it to a publisher (according to Maggy, we all know one; I don't know where she gets this absurd idea from). Next, I hope to have the joy of discovering the woman she has become, and I already feel that she will charm me even more than she did as a young girl. I will set about winning her over (please, don't mock me, it appears that, like riding a bike, we don't forget how!). And believe me, Anne-Lise, if love comes of this reunion, it will be new. I will not allow the past to steal the enchantment of discovery and uncertainty from us. Destiny does not exist, but I will pretend to believe in it . . .

Just now, coming back from the beach, Maggy and I took off our shoes and discussed the value of a grain of sand. That tiny particle that jams up the machine and alters its course. Tonight, on the verge of falling asleep, I think of you as a grain of sand, Anne-Lise, and believe me, there couldn't be a more pleasant image in my mind.

Sylvestre

P.S. Maggy wasn't mad at me about the ferns; she confessed she's used this strategy several times over the course of her walks . . .

RUE DES MORILLONS, OCTOBER 17, 2016

Dear Sylvestre,

You deserve my anger and you won't get away with it! Especially not for calling me a grain of sand when I put you back on the rails that you abandoned thirty years ago. What about your phobia of traveling? Did you forget all about it when you left, without alerting us, to cross the Breton coast? Did you think at all about how worried we might be during your relaxing strolls on the seaside?

Anyway. You've resumed your novel? It's about time! I will support you as much as possible in this endeavor. One detail I left out: the business I run with my cousin is the subsidiary of a publishing house that was created by my grandfather. That's why, Sylvestre, I am equipped to edit your book. Obviously I thought about it when I found your manuscript in the nightstand where it was waiting for me, but I forgot all about my job when I realized the value that the book held for you. So I accompanied you in this quest without any ulterior professional motive—but you knew that already.

Nevertheless, if that is your wish, I can edit your book, for no other editor will defend it with as much conviction as me. Of course, I would not take offense if you chose to hand yourself over to a stranger (but please, don't give it to my cousin!), as our friendship has no use for matters of money. The adventure I undertook at your side these last few months has no price; it was the cause of exceptional encounters with many people, the majority of whom have become friends.

Let's speak about the celebrations instead. Nahima will come with her son, William will go to Belgium to pick up Ellen Anthon and Hanne Janssen, and his daughter Laura will leave Scotland and ring in 2017 with us. David obtained his leave authorization and as you must already know, Elvire will come from Montreal on December 30 with your daughter. However, Roméo and Julie cannot join us, because they are going on a year-end trip.

It would be marvelous if you had finished your book by then, so that we have the opportunity to take a peek before you submit it to a publisher . . .

There you have it; these few words feel like a conclusion. But that's not the case. Your novel's path continues, along with your life path, and I almost envy you, you and Claire, William and Maggy, advancing on tiptoe toward an uncertain future.

But after all, isn't the future always unpredictable?

Your friend from room 128,

Anne-Lise

P.S. Despite what I insinuated above, my relations with Bastien have considerably improved since my return from Belgium. We decided to adjust our way of working together. We will go back to the way things were at the beginning, when I joined my father in the family business and he let me create the imprint that gradually became the most important of the company. I will give up a large part of the management responsibilities to my cousin (I recognize that he's getting off much better than me when it comes to money and status) and I will go back to what I do best: scouting and choosing the books that we will accompany to the shelves of bookstores and libraries to find their readers.

BELLE POELLE, DECEMBER 31, 2016

Just hours away from the new year, I am seized by an overpowering need to write. All my favorite correspondents are at my side and so I cannot send them a letter to clarify my thoughts and liberate my spirit. So I'm writing these few pages into the void, without any real recipient, like a teenager writing in her diary.

My friends and I arrived the night of December 24 and we joyously celebrated Christmas 2016. Sylvestre shared, for the first time, the end of his manuscript, which renders a vibrant homage to the young woman that Claire was thirty years ago. It must be strange to receive such a declaration of love before an audience of strangers. Fortunately for her, she could not join us in time for the public reading. She will discover this version of their story in a few months, when it adorns the shelves of bookstores. That's her wish.

To my knowledge, our two authors were very busy these last few weeks and only saw each other twice. The first time in Maggy's homeland, where Sylvestre had organized a meal at the Beau Rivage Hotel. We spoke of books and the journeys they take us on. We shared the books that have shaped our lives. William and Claire recorded the conversations on their respective phones, Maggy and Sylvestre took out small notebooks from their pockets, Agathe jotted notes in her order pad and I, I'm ashamed to say, preserved the precious advice on a paper napkin adorned with the hotel's logo . . . it's still at the bottom of my bag.

Over the course of the conversation, I observed my friends. Their faces especially. Those who were exchanging glances, those who were avoiding each other's eyes. I had an extraordinary time noting what was left unsaid and the various sneaky gestures. The brushing of fingers reaching for the pepper, the hand placed on a trembling shoulder getting up to get another helping of tart (seemingly unaware that there was still a piece on their plate) . . . Am I turning into a starry-eyed girl?

The second meeting didn't grant me as much freedom. It happened at my house on rue des Morillons, and I was so monopolized preparing the meal that I neglected the signs of complicity between my guests. When they had all left, Katia gave me her report: "Did you see how cute they are, all four of them? It's like they're afraid of admitting their feelings. Like it's too big a risk!"

We'll forgive her, she's so young . . . She knows nothing of what we stand to lose at our age when we show our cards. When the quantity of collected chips testifies to the years past and we know that there's not enough time left for us to make up for a loss. So, ever the experienced player, William keeps his distance. That grants him all of Maggy's attention, who is scared, now, to see him distance himself. She must know that her suitor is a master in the art of bluffing. But what do you expect, love is known to blind us . . .

However, I did not sense any craftiness between Sylvestre and Claire. The few gestures that they have for one another are of an infinite tenderness and they no longer hide their feelings. Perhaps they are waiting for the new year to embark on a new path side by side. If it were up to me to decide the end of the story, that is without a doubt what I would write.

From William's office, in the back of the old farmhouse, I can hear my friends' exclamations and laughter as they prepare the New Year's Eve dinner. I said I had to take a call, because I needed to isolate myself for a bit amidst the festivities. This distance allows me to savor the joy of this night all the more intensely.

For we know, you and I, how fragile perfect moments are. In a few days, Nahima will bring her son back home to his family, others will leave for Quebec or Belgium, and what will remain of our bond spurred by this book that united us? Will I still have it in my thoughts when I begin promoting the novel and Bastien and I discuss marketing and profitability? And you? Will you keep a trace somewhere of these letters and this collaboration with strangers turned friends?

I'm writing these lines to preserve the memory of all this. When

I reread them, in a week or in a year, I will rediscover the scent of the hellebore on the table for New Year's dinner and of the turkey just taken out of the oven. I will hear the laughter of Laura and Katia making fun of the adults with the cheekiness of their sixteen years, and I will see the gleam of the snow on the tops of trees surrounding the house.

Thanks to these words that will imprison these scraps of happiness, like the herbariums we make in middle school, I will finally be able to rejoin my adopted family to fully relish the celebration.

I am one of those people who cannot savor the present unless they have kept a fragment, forever nestled in the heart of their memories . . .

ACKNOWLEDGMENTS

When I say thank you, I think first of all of the people who will forever hold a place in my heart because without them, none of this would have happened.

In France, I think of the site monBestSeller.com and all its members who brought me out of the shadows almost despite myself. I think of Marie Leroy, director of the publishing house La Martinière Littérature, who was brave enough to accompany me as an inexperienced author to the front windows of bookstores. A big thank-you to Jeanne Pois-Fournier, to Sacha Serero, and to Carine Barth, who supported me by generously providing commentary, sometimes funny, always pertinent.

In the United States, I want to thank above all Marleen Seegers and Chrysothemis Armefti at 2 Seas Agency for convincing foreign editors of the value in this little French story, and of course Laura Apperson at St. Martin's Press for her enthusiasm for *The Lost Manuscript*, as well as Emma Ramadan for her fantastic translation skills. Finally, I want to thank with all my heart Sallie Lotz, my editor at St. Martin's Press, for the work she's done on the American version of this book.

Thanks to all of these people, my novel now sets off for new lands. I confess, the book didn't have such big plans. Written between April and December 2016, on the exact dates you will find within these pages, its sole ambition back then was to transport its author.

Today, incredibly, it has crossed the Atlantic and set foot on a continent I've only reached in my dreams. I hope also that you will forgive me for having used real addresses, notably in New York and Montreal. When I wrote this book, I didn't imagine it would one day find its way to you.

I will conclude by giving you, the readers, a big thank-you, for welcoming this book into your daily lives.